Morality Tale

Morality Tale

A Novel

Sylvia Brownrigg

Drawings by Monica Scott

PICADOR

First published 2008 by Counterpoint Press, Berkeley, California

First published in Great Britain 2008 by Picador

First published in Great Britain in paperback 2008 by Picador
an imprint of Pan Macmillan Ltd
Pan Macmillan, 20 New Wharf Road, London N1 9RR
Basingstoke and Oxford
Associated companies throughout the world
www.panmacmillan.com

ISBN 978-0-330-45823-8

1 3 5 7 9 8 6 4 2

A CIP catalogue record for this book is available from
the British Library.

Printed and bound in the UK by
CPI Mackays, Chatham ME5 8TD

Visit www.picador.com to read more about all our books
and to buy them. You will also find features, author interviews and
news of any author events, and you can sign up for e-newsletters
so that you're always first to hear about our new releases.

In loving memory of Mrs. Harry Batten

So heavy is the chain of wedlock that it needs
two to carry it, and sometimes three.

ALEXANDRE DUMAS

Morality Tale

Footbridge

Betrayal — It's more complicated than you think. Don't leap to conclusions. There may be hidden angles you haven't considered.

Above all, we're human. And that "we" includes you.

He told me to stop thinking about him, so I tried. Tried to clear all the thoughts of him out of my head, like clearing away the ornaments after Christmas is over, taking them down from the tree and collecting them off the ground where they've squatted in dusty nests with the pine needles and ribbon bits and unseen shavings of wrapping paper. You box them all up and put them in the basement once the festivities are over, then forget about them till next year.

That's what I tried to do with my thoughts about him.

The *he* in the first sentence is my husband. The *him* is the other guy. I had better not name *him;* it might get the man into trouble, and besides, people are more powerful if you give them names and they vanish when you don't.

He was called Richard.

There were so many things I didn't know about *him*—about

Richard. I didn't know what he liked to cook, I didn't know what books he had on his bookshelf, I didn't know how he voted. I knew he had a mom in Chicago and a dad who was dead, and a sister he liked a lot and a brother he didn't. I knew he thought the universe didn't make mistakes, which was a faith I found strange but intriguing, and I knew he believed in accepting what was and wasn't given to you, which was noble and right but at times beyond my spiritual reach. I didn't know what his mouth would feel like kissing mine, though Lord knows I imagined it. I once held his hand, that time on the park bench, and I thought of that old song about the guy with the whole world in his hands, because that's how it felt.

I guess that song is about God, though, isn't it?

I should certainly mention my husband in all of this. That was always the problem. I tried to box up my thoughts about Richard and they just wouldn't stay boxed, and I tried to get them to settle onto my husband instead and my mind, like a bird, would flutter off to a different branch altogether. It took a certain discipline, takes it still, to keep my mind focused.

He was in business. My husband. Of the two of us, he was the one with the job that tended to get referred to as "real"—as if mine were a chimera. He had a profession, though I remained womanishly vague on what it was precisely that he professed to do. He crunched numbers (like a trash compactor); he balanced books (like an acrobat). It was a position to do with finances and consulting, two words that made my mind dip into helpless narcolepsy. I could tell you that the work he did required the wearing of a suit, and that he went to an office five days out of seven, where he had a keyboard and a key card, an extension and an inbox, along with a gnawing job insecurity brought on by sinister managerial throat-clearings and co-workers he never went so far as to trust. Still, it was a job that gave him a place in the world, as jobs are meant to do, though mostly what mine gave me was standing-room only, behind the counter, next to the cash register and a handy panel of pens.

Stationery. That's where I was. It was funny, I always felt, to work in a business that was one of the nation's more common mis-spellings, and don't think I didn't occasionally get notes from friends or relatives asking how went life at the *stationary store*, like all the other stores were on the move and it was just mine that stayed still. (Cemetery is another one, I could have worked at a graveyard and been in a similar situation.) That was my station in life, my husband liked to josh with his two boys. *Pan*, as Alan and Ryan had nicknamed me long since, after some joke involving pan-demonium, *and her station at the stationery store*. Strictly speaking I had come up with the pun first—I have always enjoyed words, they are like candy or toys to me—but my husband may have forgotten that, and with everything else going on in our household it wasn't worth spending extra bitterness on questions of attribution. As Richard would have said, we have to accept what the universe has given to us, by which I supposed he meant: when your husband irritates you, you have to learn to ignore it. It was a lesson I strug-gled with.

Even now I find it difficult to go into how I met Richard, because when I think of that late-summer, near-back-to-school day it makes me happy, and I was never encouraged to be happy.

About Richard, that is. (My husband tried to press on me the importance of the distinction: he did sincerely want me to be happy, just about anything other than Richard.) After the park-bench incident with Richard and the state of emergency that followed it—our family's thankless Thanksgiving, soon succeeded by the annual joyless schedule battles over the boys' Christmas—I did my best, as per my husband's pleading demand, to find alternative sources of contentment. It wasn't easy. My sapped spirit had become so accustomed to seeking solace in that special, Richard-reserved place. It had become a Zen room in my head, a meditation chamber, a soft spot. Stepsons bratty and unmanageable? Never mind, just think about Richard. Husband recalcitrant, barking orders and complaints? That's all right, there's always Richard to think about. Worried over the mistakenness of your own paths, wrong turns taken that have made you crave distraction? One day, certainly, you ought to come to terms with all that; but for now it is easier and more enjoyable to think about Richard.

That December I worked on the problem of redirecting my thoughts. I felt like a road worker setting up one of those discouraging orange DETOUR signs right at the route you were hoping to take. It was the packed run-up to the holiday of Saint Nick, that stretch when every kind of paper product was in high demand, and at the store I waited busily on the hordes of harassed gift-givers while trying, surreptitiously, to be happy about something excluding Richard. On a rainy day, I tried to be happy that the yuletide skies gave us that calm, cleansing baptism, though as a matter of practicality it meant people were bringing in wet umbrellas all day and leaning them against the gift-wrap table where they dripped onto the rolls of printed reindeer and candy canes. I tried to be happy that the clothing-and-trinkets shop next door was playing its Christmas music so loud that every time our door opened, in blew a Winter Wonderland or jaunty, red-nosed Rudolph. My boss, Mr. Finkelstein, was a Hanukkah man himself, and drew the line at piped-in jingling and Fa-la-la-la-las. He stuck to Vivaldi to encourage the shoppers.

I tried especially hard to be happy, as my husband urged me to be, that he and I were going to the fancy Christmas dinner at the hotel up the hill, as we did every other year when the boys were not with us. (Our holidays had a binary, on/off quality in those years: with, then without; with, then without.) The hotel would serve crab cakes and lamb roast and some ice-cream confection for dessert, and we would save the cocktail stirrers for Alan and Ryan who could stab each other with them later. My husband and I would both eat and drink more than we usually did, then wonder why we came home feeling bleary and bloated. Merry Christmas, he would say with brandy on his breath, before falling into a heavy, early sleep, from which he would wake uncomfortably, around midnight, looking for Tums.

I tried these mental diversions all through that dim December, with mixed success. My thoughts seemed, devilishly, to have a mind of their own. And my husband instinctively knew it. Spouses may not yet be able to monitor all the other person's thought waves, but my husband did the job as well as he could within the limits of what was technologically possible. If I didn't laugh promptly enough at his jokes, he guessed (often correctly) that I had been listening to some inner monologue of Richard's instead.

If he caught me looking distractedly into what is literarily termed the middle distance, he assumed (mostly correctly) that my eyes were picturing Richard. If he caught me doodling on a sheet of paper, he might read the meaningless words there—FALAFEL; UNIVERSE, CHICAGO—and deduce (not incorrectly) they had something to do with that wretch of a Richard. In any of these instances, my husband would stamp or shout or hurl things around; or, worse, go very quietly gloomy, so that my heart sponged up guilt and became heavy and sodden. There was a point when it got so bad, my husband could practically read the ticker tape in my head that ran *Richard Richard Richard*, which meant I had to be careful when it came to eye contact when I was with him at home. That's one of the problems with marriage: people learn to see through you. My husband stopped being fooled by my bright, perky deflections. His gaze bored straight through all of that, searching for Richard, and more often than not finding him, to his—my husband's— despair.

I met him at the store. That was another part of the problem: we had a work connection, so my husband couldn't make stationery jokes anymore without his teeth clenching and a sound like a choked bark in the back of his throat. It was the middle of August, just after that dull, desert stretch in the midsummer calendar when there are no significant holidays. (Who sends cards for the Fourth of July? After the golf clubs and napping jokes of Father's Day there's nothing going on, date-wise, for months; the sensible people have fled town and are reading their once-a-year novels by the beach.) When mid-August rolls around we stationery employees perk up, as parents and children begin to

contemplate the end of the summer and the dawning need for sup-
plies for the new school year.

Richard was the envelope guy. The new envelope guy, I should
say, replacing hundred-year-old Milton, a specimen whose face
had been lined by his long, dedicated years of correspondence-
enhancing salesmanship. There was nothing you could tell Milton
about envelopes that he didn't already know. The man breathed
envelopes. For all I knew, he ate them.

Richard was not like that. He knew envelopes, yes, dimensions,
colors and weights, and he could talk for a surprising number of
minutes on the padded-versus-not-padded question. If you showed
him a piece of paper of any irregular size, he would find you an envelope that neatly contained it, and he went to some lengths to prove
the superiority of envelopes over boxes for most mailings. He could
even, if you asked, give you the derivation of the name "Manila."

But none of that really interested him. I understood that immediately, that there was more to Richard than mere envelopes.
Richard was a man who loved people and who loved stories. He
was at heart a philosopher, in the narrative school. His real passion
was for the cosmos and its workings: the stars and the planets, and
why we are here. He was the kind of guy who read plenty of science fiction, which put him in touch with a great number of other
universes, the parallel and the not-so-parallel both.

"So you're the new envelope guy," I said when I met him on a
Monday morning that fateful, fitful August. The skies were unpre-
dictable, you could not know when or whether the cold morning
fog would lift, and my moods, I'll admit, had become similar: there
were days when I kept waiting for the sun and good humor to

break through but they just never did. My remark to the new man was something of a redundancy—Richard had appeared alongside our most recent shipment of envelopes, to make my and Mr. Finkelstein's acquaintance—but I was trying to be friendly.

"That's right," Richard said, and there was elastic in his voice. Springiness. Life. "Richard Applebee. Pleased to meet you. You may think of me as an envelope pusher, but I like to think of myself as someone who pushes the envelope." He chuckled like a hen.

The line did not have the fresh flavor of something the man had just thought up on the spot; it had more of the ziplocked staleness of something he had put together earlier and was now carrying around for new clients or friends. That was all right with me, though. We can't always be original, every time. It would be far too tiring.

"Which envelope do you push?" I asked Richard. I liked him right away. His voice was warm and his eyes were alight. He gave the impression of fullness: he was quietly hefty, with a rounded rusty beard and pink-leaning skin. An Irish Santa Claus, maybe. Somebody whose suit buttons didn't really want to stay closed. Isn't attraction mysterious? My husband was on the slim side, something I had considered a virtue, proof that he didn't get carried away with his appetites—though the earlier part of our history might have suggested otherwise. And facial hair! I had never in my life thought the stuff was appealing, the way it made men's skin so furry and primitive. Nuzzling against the undergrowth: wouldn't it be like kissing a marmoset? Yet here I was, watching the orange steel wool scrubbing this man's clean, shiny face, and thinking it might be nice to put my cheek against that texture. And all this before I knew the first thing about him.

"Well," Richard answered me, glancing at his notes, "I see you have a standing order for the McKinleys in nine by twelve and ten by thirteen, and I don't see any reason to suggest—"

"No, no." I think it was then that I touched a couple of fingers to his sweatered arm. This boldness was unusual for me. Maybe I was testing, instinctively, to see whether he was real, or a mirage. Maybe I was wondering if I had somehow dreamt him. "I meant— which envelope do you push, generally?" And I gestured, with a flourish, at the wider world, a world beyond stationery.

"Oh!" The carrot-headed man put his notes down on the counter between us, and I could see from his face he liked the question. I was taking his joke seriously. I was trying to open him up. "I mean, I enjoy looking at things from an angle. Thinking out-side the box. I consider myself a person who marches"—now his voice sounded shy, endearingly so, in spite of his size and his beard—"to the beat of a different drummer." That was his small speech. He put his hands together and rested them on the counter. The melamine might as well have been an altar, the way I felt at that moment, and the receipt for the envelopes, a ring. I was ready to follow this man, this big man, to someplace else. Someplace far away, someplace different. I, too, was eager to get out of the damned box; my own had become so airless and miserable lately.

That was the size and shape of our first encounter. We talked a little more that day, but honestly, not much. He was conscious of keeping to his schedule, meeting all the people who for years would have known only Milton, and I, meanwhile, had the typical stream of humanity coming in needing its staple guns and tape dispensers, its Post-Its and paperclips. While Richard was still in the store, for instance, a troubled man came in searching for an envelope to fit his child's passport. The passport had to be sent upstate to the child's mother so that mother and child could go on a trip to Mexico, which the father didn't approve of. (Divorce and its dramas: they're everywhere you look. Is there anyone untouched?) People used to offer these stories about themselves even when you didn't much want to hear them, and I was good enough at my job that I listened while customers gave the backstory of their particular requests. I was frustrated that it cut off the conversation with my new friend, the plain-suited St. Nick, but on the other hand it meant he got to see me in action. Perhaps I was showing off for Richard as I helped find a container for the customer's travel anxiety; it was an envelope question, after all. We settled on a number four, padded, and I sensed Richard's approval. (My husband, on the other hand, had not seen me perform in this way in a long while. He had not taken in that there were items at the stationery store I was quite skilled at selling.) By the time the guy, now calmer, was gone, I could see in Richard's four-leaf-clovered eyes a glitter of respect and curiosity. "I hope we have chances to talk further," he said rather formally, before he left, but I was fairly sure the formality was a thin cover for shyness.

I thought about Richard's hope that evening as I made my slow-footed way back to my husband, and to the worn-down lives we were worn out from living: the ones in which I'd pick up the remaining morning debris as I always did, cook some form of dinner as I always did, listen as I always did to my husband's tense

uncoilings about work. It was a short journey home from the stationery station, past the shoe shop and the bookstore and the colorful perfumed cave that sold clothes from Tibet, back to our
bike-and-skateboardy neighborhood, where the leaders of tomorrow made their first helmeted attempts to weave and maneuver
without crashing. As I walked, I considered the possibility of there
being chances to *talk further* with the big red-haired gentleman I
had met from Envelopes Incorporated, and how unlikely it was
that there would ever be any. The truth was, Richard Applebee
wouldn't have much reason to stop by the store, in a professional
capacity—shipping services would do the talking, for the most
part; it wasn't a horse-and-cart world in which he himself needed
to swing by with the goods. And my own geographies had become
so limited: overpriced health mart, where I picked up ingredients
for two or for four, depending on the calendar; the children's
school for collection of the boys, depending on same; bookstore
for reading material, without which so little is bearable; post office
to send checks for our accumulated parking tickets and periodi-
cally mail missives to my dear, far-away mother. Oh, and every
now and then a jaunt to the marriage counselor's office, when my
husband's ex-wife Theresa (DDT, or Dear Darling Terry, as we
sometimes called her, our little joke) had pushed one of us over
some edge, and we needed the cool unflappability of Dr. Puffin to
steady us. Really, that just about covered it. You see how small my
particular circuit had gotten to be.

It was hard to imagine Richard popping up in any of those
places, though don't think I wasn't thinking about it the next day
as I wheeled a cart up and down the overstuffed aisles of the

holier-than-thou health mart, performing the twenty-first-century version of hunting and gathering. I hacked through the jungle of brand names, choosing healthy but fun cereal for the boys in boxes decorated with facts about the world's waning wildlife, and selecting pasta made of colorful compressed vegetables designed to sneak nutritional content past fussy eaters' taste buds. Up and down I pushed my cart like a baby pram while rehearsing the spontaneous, joyful greeting that would take place before banks of green and black olives, or out near the nut butters. "Why, Mr. Applebee!" I'd say. (It is regrettable that you can't choose the names of the people you fall for; *Richard* was unobjectionable, but *Applebee* had the scent of cartoon to it, I couldn't deny it.) Yet that was his name, and like the color of his hair not something he could help. "Why, Mr. Applebee," I'd say. "Hello! And here you are, marching. How is your drummer?"

Too forced?

"Hello again—aren't you Mr. Applebee, the man who pushes the envelope?"

"Richard," he'd correct me, warmly. That was something I had noticed about him almost immediately—his warmth. When he left that first day, he had clasped my small, cautious hand in his, and I had the fleeting sensation that here was someone who could whisk me away with him, who could take me far off from the mess of my life. Who knows why such an idea strikes you about someone you just met? A touch, even a brief one, can hold so much. That hand-clasp contained everything—a story, an excitement, a world—and the phantom feeling came back to me as I wandered the aisles, hoping I'd see him.

However. What I actually saw, over in condiments, was a familiar brown-helmet-haired woman, with a face that was drawn like a
queen's—proud, stern, and baffled, as if disappointed by her subjects. The woman was contemplating ketchups. For all I knew she
was making the same kind of food-provider decisions I was (how
to strike a balance between healthy and tasty? Was there a way to
avoid paying over the odds for such staples?), but in any case it was
not the poignancy of the similarity between us that struck me. The
important point was that she must not see me. Etched still into my
eyelids—and for that matter my eardrums—was the shape and
sound of Theresa's shattering cry of years earlier, when she once
caught sight of me at the entrance to said health mart, with Ryan
pattering along innocently behind me. *"NO!"* she had shrieked
simply, a denial of such vehemence and violence that it tore up the
climate-controlled air and shredded the nerves of the shoppers all
around us. The boy was petrified and confused. The clock
stopped. It was hard to recover.

From that point on I elected to do my shopping alone.

So, noticing her there, parsing mustards, I retreated—away
from the mercifully unaware Theresa and her crouched, attendant
hysteria, back toward the checkout and my Richard-fed day-
dreams. It was a sunnier place to be, by far, though I recognized
that the whole notion of a health-mart encounter with Richard
was based on the wobbly premise that he might live near enough
to us that he'd have reason to frequent that same institution, with
its jacked-up prices and feel-good interior, its purified half-hourly
water spritz over the gleaming green vegetables. While in fact
one reason I was so drawn to Richard, doubtless, was that he had a

distant air about him, the whiff of coming from somewhere quite else. He was in all likelihood not an inhabitant of our own constricted, suffocated, several-blocks quarter, that stretch of acreage that had become something like an urban dog run for me— fenced-in and colorless, without the cheer or freedom of a genuine park. Richard probably, I reflected, lived up the freeway or down from my husband and me, maybe even across one of the bridges. He might live on the other side of the water altogether, in a place where the air seemed cleaner and trees crowded round generously, and the nearby mountain conferred nobility on everyone in its shadow—even the rich and the foolish, of whom there were plenty.

It was years since I had been there myself, to that town across the bay. I grew up there, under the skyscraper-high redwoods, in the fragrant groves of bay laurels. It was there that my mother and I had once lived, and where we had befriended our kind, diamond-hearted neighbor Millie, who was like a grandmother to me. I had been meaning to go back for a visit, but with the many demands of my husband and Alan and Ryan and the largely invisible but unstoppable DDT I had not managed it. The town might no longer be peopled and alive for me as it had been, but I had griefs lodged over there. Histories. Markers. We each of us have our private geographies of mourning, and that place, by the mountain, was one of mine.

But I would prefer not to go down that thorny, overgrown path just now, the one that leads to memories of loss and abandonment. Let me instead remind myself that it was my husband, bless him, with his pleasant, clean-shaven face—the kind of face that could

sell you life insurance or all-wool carpeting, in natural colors—
who pulled me away from the particular darkness I inhabited when
he first met me; who, like a strong swimmer, hauled me to shore,
sodden maiden in distress that I was. I was miles away from all
those old mountain shadows by then, but I'm sure you don't need
me to tell you that physical and mental distances are immeasurably
different. That, for instance, the guy rejected by the only person
he ever loved, a farm girl in Wyoming, might try to forget about
her by traveling to India, only to find himself up on some peak
staring at the dusky azure Himalayas, with his girl's voice in his
head and an overwhelming sense memory of the taste of her
pound cake. There is no way to escape it: these things follow you.
Dreams, yes, and demons, and the ugly snake of regret that coils at
times around your heart, leaving you breathless.

That was me, stuck, helpless, when my husband discovered me,
back in my café-going days. I had the fanciful idea that I was writing a book—my Dictionary of Betrayal, I called it—a collection of
words and their meanings that would gradually build a story, a
world. Betrayal, Abandonment, Grief; Sex, Lying, Revenge. There
was plenty of material. It was a slow dirge of a project, admittedly.
It had me going in circles around actions I could not undo, trying
to rewrite dramas whose scripts had already been played out. Sitting in a café with a pad of paper and a pen (I was, myself, quite a
consumer of stationery products) allowed me to steam in my own
juices, which may be what you want for a pot roast but is not the
best thing for a person given to overly morose introversions.

To his lasting credit, my husband understood this. Quickly,
instinctively. He was capable, in those clear days before the chaos

and tantrums (before the *NO!*s, the *how dare you*s, the *get the boys out here, right now!*s), of bright moments of perception when he turned his focus to me. He saw me. He took me in. When he found me scribbling in the café, what he saw was a muddled someone who needed the pen taken away from her for a while, the notebook retired to a high shelf out of sight, out of mind, a steady masculine arm to lean on as she tottered up and down the avenue. "I want to keep you like a key," he used to tell me, in a voice that soothed so. "I want to put you in my pocket. I want to hold you close, make you safe, calm, and happy."

He did not have the idea, thank goodness, to replace the notebook and pen with a baby and diaper—there are some men (and women too, for that matter) who would have made that trade, but for him and me both, life seemed complicated enough without the extra patter of little feet around. Perhaps what would serve me best, he felt, would be a low-stress position at a nearby harmless enterprise like the stationery store. Stationery was always supposed to be temporary, a way station, but it turned into something quite different, and, like many elements of our first few years (divorce warfare, intense lovemaking, political disillusionment), lasted longer than expected.

He imagined leading me out of my darkness, my husband, even as he first stood by my table holding a hot cappuccino, not yet mine at all. Later, he tended to tell the story in simpler terms: he said that when he saw me in my blue scarf and gray shirt, my pale cheeks and rosehip lips, he wanted to kiss me. And from there, that café moment, our story unfolded, with the heavy inevitability that clings to encounters of people who wind up getting married.

I always found it worse thinking about all that murk, our beginnings, than it ever was to think about Richard, whether or not thoughts about him were banned, and even when I was trying my damnedest to cleanse the man from my palate. My guess after a certain point was that it was useless, that Richard was just stuck there, like a piece of corn in the molars or the so-called fresh taste of toothpaste, though the latter could, in my opinion, carry with it the hint of guilt (as in, what other lurking flavor was a person trying to conceal?).

Water under the bridge, people say, to cover events in your life you might like to forget about or change, like marrying a man who meant well and saved you, in one sense, only to ruin you, in a different, spiritual one. Water under the bridge. What does it mean? You have a picture of yourself standing on a footbridge over a river, like the one I used to walk my dog across when I was a teenager; the dog would scurry on over into the park to meet his dog friends and acquaintances, while I paused on the bridge a moment, watching the flow of the water, only vaguely aware at the time of its metaphorical richnesses. Too young yet to have made large mistakes that I could imagine I was watching float along on the river under my feet. Back then it was all still in the future; the present was mostly a packed catalog of predictable adolescent embarrassments. Oh, there were winces of shame, sure, but they were in relation to saying something dumb to a cute boy in Physics, or rashly waving hello at a popular girl who might feign not to have seen me. At fifteen you're not yet talking about holocausts of the heart or severe moral lapses, the deep troubled issues of character which, when it comes to your private consultations with God or your conscience, whichever one you believe in, are all that actually matter.

So I could watch the water of my marriage rush past, or perhaps the marriage was a twig on top of the water caught in the flow of the river, and I could see it travel beneath and then beyond me, moving quickly downstream where I would never catch up with it. I could never take it back; my husband and I were destined to keep going together, as we had from the ill-planned beginning, on down and down, far past the footbridge. And so is it any wonder, if I was thinking of it that way, that there were long hours over stationery, when my husband couldn't see me, that I mooned over Richard, pondering the big man's words and his philosophies, the alternative he offered?

It is important, when you're reckoning (with God or your conscience, whichever one you believe in), to stand up and tell the truth. That much we all know from grade school, where the punishments were less severe for those who stepped forward and confessed. If you hold on to secrets they build up interest, like savings accounts, gathering more wickedness around them and doing more damage. Our nation's president learned this rather publicly in the seventies, when I was an impressionable youth. I watched the false-smiling politician on TV as he worked out that no wall was high or strong enough to keep out nosy, persistent reporters. The taller you tried to build the thing, the louder the crash at the end. Watergate made a mark on me as on everybody, I guess. One of my keenest memories was of once saying to my mother, "I wish the president was dead!" in a precocious attempt to win approval for my political stance, since I knew she loathed the man—only to be told how deeply wrong that was, as a wish. My mother chastised me in no uncertain terms. It was my first remembered instruction in separating a person from the deed they commit; my first understanding that you must not wish someone dead, however much you despise them.

He was married when I met him, that was the problem. My husband, I mean. You couldn't tell that about him—he didn't wear a ring, not that I was ever one of those people who notice rings (later my own would be demure and only lightly diamonded, as I felt the big rocks looked garish and nervous). He seemed like a regular guy, my husband, standing there with his cappuccino and a slightly hungry expression, though already there was a vibration about him that suggested a wish and a willingness—for story, for excitement, maybe. Still, I half thought he was simply getting ready to make a speech about life insurance or wool carpeting. I was naive and also not, in those days; innocent on the surface with a cunning ooze within, like a dark smooth chocolate with cherry liqueur hidden inside. I suppose I could see that he liked me, but I was willing to persuade myself that it was for all the right reasons. Besides, I didn't know he was married.

It was only on the third cappuccino that that detail came up. This was the third lunchtime in a row he had come into the café and discovered me at my dictionary (I put a protective arm over the notebook when he came up, not that my scrawl is so legible, but you hardly want entries on Abandonment and Cheating jumping off the page into the sightlines of someone you're just getting to know). He was taking his midday break from the office where he did finances or consulting, or both (my brain jellied even then when he tried to explain it). And I responded to this man, deeply: he reminded me of someone kind I had once known, or imagined I had known, or would have liked to know. He had an old-world sturdiness. Internal, I mean. He was a man who knew what was what. When you're rudderless, as I was then, there is an appeal in that certainty. I was in a wavery, irregular state at the time, like a kid's mobile with the strings tangled, dangly and awkward. My to-be husband saw that about me, and wanted to fix it.

Why was I broken? I would have to go back some ways to explain it. Back to mistakes made even earlier, on the other side of the bay, abandonments committed, losses suffered or allowed. I don't want to give you the whole list. Suffice it to say that when a man approached me who wanted to keep me like a key, and put me in his pocket, I was happy to let him. When he told me he was married but on the brink of separation, the bond with his wife long since severed, I was willing to believe it. When he shared his view that nothing could be more damaging for children than to grow up in a loveless, hostile atmosphere, I was inclined to agree.

There was nothing, my husband breathed, in the intervals between the hot, sloppy kisses that started up between us, that should get in the way of us holding each other, there and then. We were destined to be together, my husband and me, we were (to hear him tell it) already water under the bridge. I should not question or fight it. I should simply give in to his strong arms and his conviction, his powerful belief that we were meant for each other.

So I did.

Plaid Living-room Set

Stains — Out, out, damn'd spot! Remember that?
That was a good one.

—

Nobody wants to be a second wife. It's nobody's great ambition in life, to inhabit days loud with shouted schedule conflicts, telephones slammed down or cursed into, cars speeding away with the hysterical exclamation point of burnt rubber. It's not what you dream of for yourself when you're a lively teenager, say, writing essays, playing volleyball (one of the great team sports), or walking your dog across footbridges under overcast skies. Though if you'd ever stopped to do the math—and you were always good at math—you'd have been able to figure it out: in a country where a divorce occurs every thirty seconds, there will be a sizable number of divorcers getting remarried. Therefore, second wives. If it turns out to be you, if that's the straw you happen to draw—tough luck. You're never going to get the kind of joy you might have hoped for when you walk into a marriage that used to belong to somebody else. It's like moving into a new house that still has half the previous owner's furniture in it. You'd like to get rid of the all-plaid living-room set, but somehow you're stuck with it, forever.

In my case, the plaid living-room set was called Theresa.

She hated me. Theresa. She thought I ruined her life, smashed up a family, stole something that wasn't mine; she thought, therefore, that I should go to jail, or Siberia, or hell, whichever would cause me most agony. (Hell, probably, right? All those flames. Plus, it lasts longer.) Through the years, I had thought about going to any one of those places—rather wistfully, since they had to be more comfortable and appropriate (even hell, in its overheated way) than where my husband and I were that entire time, namely in a small condo just one side of the health mart, on the other side of which resided Theresa and the boys, scraping out a father-free living.

Alan and Ryan. He told me about them one day at the café where we met; the whole situation came out in a rush: *I've-got-a-coupla-kids-but-am-just-about-separated-from-my-wife*. It was the content of that "just about" that had proved so contentious, since the then-wife, Theresa, would swear on a stack of wedding vows that she and her then-husband had never discussed sundering and were still quite united. But the way this clean-faced man delivered the news of his marriage to me, it was like he was talking about a timeshare in the Sierras or that beat-up old station wagon he'd been meaning to get rid of. Some item that was part of his general inventory, but not something I needed to worry overly over—he'd quietly offload it somewhere discreet. He was a fixer, this guy. He would sort it all out for us. My job, as the pretty one, the one with the nice lips, was simply to kiss him, to embrace him, to fall into his arms. To believe him. So I did.

He was never a heartless father, my husband. In his distractible, hapless way he loved those two boys, and went to some pains to insist that they would be better off growing up without that particular vexed, torn-up first marriage over their heads (it provided such poor shelter). But it would be fair to call him old-school in the fathering department—he wasn't one of those bouncy modern men who lined the streets around where we lived, wearing babies in pouches around their necks like medals brought back from some war, pushing double strollers with virile elegance and ease. We had a lot of that around our neighborhood. I used to see them all around, dads buying scones for demanding toddlers, speaking in dulcet tones to try to win childish compliance. (It didn't, I noticed, work very well for them either.) My husband was more traditional, in the "I'll throw a football with you and buy you clock radios" line, leaving many of the finer points of hygiene and wardrobe procurement to the boys' mother. When it came time for the lawyers to carve up Alan and Ryan's calendar, like slicing the holiday turkey, my husband volunteered to take the brown meat, the gristle—a couple of school days, including the ones on which they had their infernal sports practices, and every other weekend. For my part I found the series of days hard to digest, but it was hardly for me to comment or complain.

Here's what happens: you find yourself taken by strong, comforting arms away from someplace dark and unhappy, and you're grateful, you're soothed, you are lulled by the difference into a spiritual complacency. There you were, working away madly on a putative dictionary, sipping too much rosehip tea and trying to avoid the inevitable thoughts about loss, when a friendly person swept you off to someplace full of chatty nights and sweet gifts, eggs in the morning and the warming gleam of adoration. Those arms took you to a safe haven, or so you thought, some location strangely, improbably secure, and you sank into the feeling like diving into a soft, colorful pile of leaves. And it took you a couple of years to notice that under the colorful leaves was the hardest cement all along, that your limbs were sore and bruised, and your sense of self battered. That those loving arms, promise laden, were not able to break your hard fall.

My husband tried to blast us past those inconveniences. He wanted to be like the guy in the action movie who clutches the girl to him, carrying her beyond the snakes, bullets, and explosions, till they end up in some atmospheric shelter together, where he can brush the hair from her forehead and murmur, "Are you all right, my darling?" For the first noisy months that had been my husband's plan. These were the noisy months that came after the sultry, secretive months, when those sloppy hot kisses I mentioned took place behind the closed doors of my shabby apartment, and this man, my lover, was performing the complex choreography of the cellphone, in which he alternately ignored the device, turned it off, or answered and lied into it. This was not edifying to watch, though it did provoke reflections on how different adultery must have been in the olden days, when we were not able to track one another with the ruthless precision we have now, chasing our loved ones with queries and ringtones. Trust must have been a great airy balloon in those days, light and round and full of mystery, because the weeks would have long hours in them during which you'd have no expectation of speaking with your spouse or beloved (if these happened to be one and the same person). A few years from now infidelity will be even more of a challenge, as jealous partners the world over will implant chips in the other's wrist so they can monitor his or her geographies on a screen set up in the bedroom. If my husband could have done that with me, after the contrivances with Richard had been discovered, he would have. But that remark takes us back to Richard, and I'm not ready to return to him. It is so much jollier picking over the colorful good intentions that paved my own path to hell.

Because you have to ask yourself, don't you, what was this girl thinking, listening to the guy lie like that to his wife? Wasn't that approximately the point at which this girl might have called the "just about separated from" line into question? Does a man really need to hedge and prevaricate to a woman if their marriage has ended (she might have wondered)? If this man was the rosehip girl's knight in bright armor, and being together was their romantic, windswept destiny, wasn't it a shame that the horse he rode in on wasn't white, but was in fact rather stained and grey, mottled with the marks of his self-serving deceptions and distortions?

Everyone is flawed, no doubt about it, and no one looks his best when skulking out of a marriage. But what about the other person in the picture, the princess, the babe with the damp lock of hair on the forehead, the younger heroine? (Because I was younger than DDT, a fact that contributed in no small part to her hatred.) She, the babe, the princess, the heroine—*me*—doesn't look very good, either. She, let's be honest here, does not look too good.

One of the boys asked me a question one day. Theresa's boys. My husband's boys. Alan and Ryan, at ten and twelve they were pretty well alike, both dark-haired blurs of video games, home-work, and jokes about flatulence. One of them asked me a sneaky kid question—it was probably Alan, he was the older one and try-ing then to discern the shape of laws and rules, and how he might find a way round them. This was what Alan asked me: If you don't know a law exists, can you still get into trouble for breaking it? Maybe we were passing a NO TRESPASSING sign, or a DO NOT RIDE YOUR BIKE ON THE PATH sign, and Alan could picture himself pedal-ing along, defying the edict. Could he plead ignorance? "You still get into trouble," I told him crisply, trying to play the role of authority. I didn't want him biking where he wasn't supposed to bike, or treading on the property of someone who might come after him with a shotgun. "Maybe just not quite as much."

When I used to conceive of myself actually talking to Mother Theresa (another humorous name I had for her)—when I some-how thought we might get past the point where she spat venom in my eye, or lunged the dagger of long-imagined revenge into my heart—I considered using that line of defense. *I didn't know. I had only one half of the story to go on.* I didn't know the marriage wasn't over, because he said it was, and honestly he was quite convincing. If I'd had you to talk to at the time, Theresa, no doubt I'd have heard something different, because in a marriage there are at least two, if not dozens, of sides to each story. A marriage is in its way like a faceted disco ball, covered with scores of small angled mir-rors, each one reflecting back a different shard of the narrative to whoever's looking at it.

But I'm not sure that Theresa and I would get all that far with *I didn't know*. Because it would be truer to say to Theresa that the person who presented himself to me was not enacting the role of someone who was married. The man who stood with the cappuccino, before sitting down cautiously to talk in mild tones with a young woman he suddenly wanted to kiss, a woman with a shy smile who seemed ever so slightly unhinged, the way she was scribbling—anyway, that man was thinned out and hollow and wore a hunger on his face that you could read as easily as the café menu posted in white chalk up on the chalkboard. (*Latte, macchiato, cappuccino, espresso*, our latterday lyric of the siren song of caffeine.) He was aching for affection. For friendship. For conversation. In other words, while this kind man with the strong arms felt the urge to save *me*, I have to say that I had the distinct impression that he was a man who, in his own way, also needed rescue. He was all dried up, out of love, hadn't been touched or held in some god-awful number of years now. (This was something he told me.) What I wanted to do was bring this restorable man back to life and liquidity, pour energy into his limbs, refresh that good, dehydrated heart, remind him as no one had for a long while that he was good-looking, desirable, a hero. I wanted to help him, too.

And after lunch turned to dinner turned to a movie turned to kissing, my desire, which sounds benevolent enough when I put it that way, turned more specific, as desires in their determined way tend to do, and shaped up as a want for his particular muscular arms, his love-sonnet phrases, his hot, sloppy kisses, and above all, the entangling that follows such kisses. The lack of bulk in his form I found attractive then, and though I now describe my husband as cold-ish, in those days the thermostat was turned up high. And his hunger matched mine: mine matched his. In that respect he was right, we were well matched, and what kind of wife has a husband so famished, so lonely, so free in his heart to wander into a café and fall over cappuccino in love with a rosehip-lipped girl? What kind of woman could Theresa have been, to empty the man out so? True, I didn't know her story, her griefs and her pains, but what I did know, because actions are much louder than words, was that her hold on the person she had married must have some time since been released. Her love, her attention had drifted elsewhere. They certainly had not touched her husband for years. Her eyes, heart, hands had probably been—mothers do this of course, happens all the time—with her children, and she hoped the husband, like a rock garden, might take care of himself, need no tending.

If all of us wicked second wives held a conference, I guess that would probably be the keynote speech. Well, You Let Him Go, Didn't You? (And across the busy boulevard at a competing hotel is the parallel conference, for first wives, with panels entitled He Done Me Wrong and That Dog: I Burned All His Clothes, and several dedicated to the topic of Our So-Called Sisters, Those Other Women: How Could They Do It?) Martyrdom is all very well, ladies, but let's face it: You let him go. You neglected him to the point of desiccation and withering, and that's how I found him. Don't be surprised that a guy parched for attention would stop, somewhere, for a drink.

I was thinking about all this with new poignancy that winter because I could see that the same thing had happened, in a sense, with Richard (though I was not supposed to think or talk about Richard). I remembered my husband discovering the stash of little notes Richard had sent to me, along with the envelope shipments—it had become a thrilling part of my week, opening up boxes from Envelopes Incorporated to see what personal salutation Richard had left in there for me to discover, like hunting for Easter eggs. My husband tore out his peppery brown hair over Richard's statements of esteem and affection (for me; for *me!*), saying, or more accurately howling, "How could you let this bulbous clown send you mash notes? Were you encouraging him? *What was going on here?*"

And secretly, inside myself, where he couldn't hear me, because I was too scared to utter the statement to him directly, I said to my husband: Doesn't it make you wonder how unhappy I had become at home, in our windswept, destined life together, if I could be open-hearted in this way to a warm philosophical gentleman who does not, to my eye, resemble a clown? Doesn't it make you worry about how untouched *I* was, if the envelope guy could put his hand on mine and I'd feel newly alive? We're talking five years into the marriage now—ours, that is, my husband's and mine—and the hot sloppy kisses had turned drier and tidier some time before. And so I had arms eager for Richard, arms that could reach across the melamine counter for the words and friendship of some guy who thought outside the box and made bad jokes about pushing the envelope, all because I had a kind of hollow, a need, and it seemed to me he might fill it. Does that, I would have asked my husband if I was feeling brave, remind you of anybody? Does the story ring a bell at all? Sound anything like a guy with a cappuccino who walked into a café a little over five years ago, looking for a jolt of caffeine to keep him going through the work morning and discovering instead some girl he wanted to kiss, save, and marry?

What goes around comes around, in the soothing nonsensical wisdom of the ages. I thought that about Richard, about my feelings for him, when I allowed them to wash over me if I was alone in the bathroom, door locked, shower running. (That was where it was safest to go with my thoughts about Richard.) I recalled that carousel of a saying. What goes around comes around.

We married with her curses flying overhead like paparazzi helicopters. ("One day, I swear, she'll leave you just like you left me, for somebody else! Your sons will never forgive you! I hope to God you end up old and alone!") We had assembled a small group of partisan friends at the ceremony—people likely to cheer, or at least nod approvingly, rather than mutter and point. Because even the friends of the second-marryers have to take some sort of position on the uncomfortable orientation of the thing. It's an awkward situation for the attendee of that kind of wedding. How can you full-heartedly weep and believe in the new union when the feast meats of the first one's funeral haven't yet gone cold (to paraphrase Hamlet)? You can proclaim your dislike of the first wife, but that looks churlish and uncharitable, even if the woman does have a sour mouth and a dagger tongue and lacks the habit of smiling unless strictly necessary. You can not have known her, of course, and thus plead ignorance, like Alan riding his bicycle along the proscribed path. This was the land staked out by my mother, whose maternal heart struggled over whether to be proud or ashamed of her daughter's marriage to a man who had kids, an ex-wife, and a suburban house he was vacating to inhabit a smaller, morally compromised condo with me. (If our neighbor Millie had still been alive, she would have helped my mother settle herself;

she would have known how to make her feel comfortable—
content, even.) It caused a pain somewhere between my stomach
and my heart to see my mother's face rippled with a confusion of
sentiments: relief, anxiety, and hope, mingled with something
murkier, like suspicion; what did my daughter do to take this man
away from his wife? She never uttered that question, but it was
legible in her squinting eyes, on her frowning brow, as she stood in
the half-shadows of the nuptial party.

Others took a different tack. These tended to be the ones who
did know Theresa, who had seen the plaid living-room set in situ.
Judging from what I heard, she was not a pretty sight, though if the
words *shrew* or *harridan* ever surfaced in my mind I batted them away
as sexist and probably unfair. (If I mention that the boys had the
facial twitch of children yelled at frequently by a bad-tempered
parent, you might or might not be inclined to believe me.)
Anyway, the people on my husband's side who came with their
high kicks and pom-poms to cheerlead him into his next match up,
his sequel, had behind them the handy late-modern fatalism about
matrimony. What can you do? Some marriages just don't last, the
couple didn't make sense in the first place, and let's hope—RAH!
—that the guy's gotten it right this time. Let's hope this is the one
for him. The first choice was misguided, after all, and if they've got
two children to show for it, well that's a shame, no question, for
the kids, but luckily there are tons of good books out there to help
with the tricky logistics and emotional minefields of joint custody.
And, if it comes to it, there are a hell of a lot of professionals waiting with offices lined with board games and sandboxes for the children, and neutral, inoffensive prints on the walls, and boxes of

Kleenex on the side tables, for the adults. They'll meet you and reassure you and coach you through your bitterness and arrangements. The bill will come separately.

In a country as crammed with divorce as this one, you've got to figure there are hundreds of people out there each week making the above kind of speech to accommodate some pal of theirs who's retying the knot, or rather tying a different knot, hoping this new one will hold better, not snap or fray. *Good luck this time, Bob! Fingers crossed, eh? I never much liked the other one anyway.* The sappier, possibly feminine version of which is, *You two are perfect together, I'm so glad you found each other. That's what's important, that you found each other* now—*no need to dwell on what came before.* Not that you'll be able to forget it, of course, because the children of the first union will assail you, those living, growing incarnations of the plaid living-room set.

They were there that day, too, Alan and Ryan, over Theresa's dead body as she snarled when the suggestion was first put to her, but sadly it didn't work out that way; the boys were dragged along to take part and DDT lived on to fight another day. They were young guys at the time, still cute and head-pattable, and some benign aunt put them in suits like they were going to church, which they weren't; my husband and I weren't that sacrilegious, and they, Alan and Ryan (they tended to blur together; both were brown haired and blunt nosed and evaded my glance), sat at the back of the old boat club—venue selected by my husband, to symbolize, I suppose, our great new launch on life's rocky waves. Anyway, Alan and Ryan sat at the back and played cards and ate candy, the time-honored sugar bribe provided by their dad. As I've said, he wasn't the most progressive father in all respects, but it was important to my husband that his offspring be there on the occa-sion of his supposedly getting it right, finally, in relation to his matrimonial destiny. Sorry, boys, about your mother, that was a regrettable mistake. Here's my do-over. The boys didn't offer an opinion; how could they? They sat at the back with their candy bars, playing War. It was the best you could hope for.

And me? Sparkly white from my pure virginal head down to my clean, innocent toes? I don't think so. I'm still reluctant to drag up the other sordid histories of my life before I met my husband, the various betrayals that prompted me to start writing my dic-tionary in the first place. But I can demurely tell you that if wear-ing a big red A on my wedding dress would have seemed somewhat old-fashioned, conceding perceptual ground to the enemy, then neither would a snow-white gown have seemed quite like truth in advertising. I settled for a kind of burned-gold color: something bright and shiny to denote my sense that this was a jeweled occasion (or so we hoped), but a shade dark enough to hide or absorb any stains, moral or otherwise. My husband seemed pleased with the choice, though he did not, I think, understand the subtleties that went into it. He wore black—it's always easier for men—and a crisp white shirt underneath it, blemishless, because as he said over and over to me then and in the years after, he did not feel guilt. Theresa had left him long since, in love if not in letter, leaving him free to be reawakened by somebody else. In my husband's opinion he and I might both have worn garments the hue of summer clouds and, with our excellent intentions, been above reproach.

That's how he carried himself that entire day, and I admired him for it. He stood lean and upright and beaming, his shoulders straight, his head steady, no sign in his bright eyes that he felt any dark currents on the air—just a glowing blush warming his face, as if he were the bride, not I. Everything about his expression and his body wore the conviction that he was doing us both an enormous favor, introducing us to our destiny, and that he fully expected only congratulations and praise for his efforts. "I'm a lucky man," he said to anyone who would listen. "She's a wonder, isn't she? I'm a lucky man today."

But what was the bride like? That's what people always want to know. How did she look? Was she beautiful? Was it the happiest day of her life, better even than going to Disneyland when she was nine and thrilling to the spinning teacups and the Matterhorn, the small world after all? (That last is still a standout day in my history, actually. That and the day our volleyball team won the regional championships.)

He carried me through it. I can say that about my husband, with his strong arms and his determination: the horse he was riding on may have been mottled, but he rode high and he rode proud.

Meanwhile, every time I saw those diminutive chocolate-crunching card players I thought of their mother's fervent hope that they would loathe me forever, and one day plan patricide to avenge their mother's betrayal. They, the boys themselves, seemed vague, a bit bewildered, mostly just trying to get through one more grownup charade together. The benign aunt shepherded them around, which allowed her not to feel she had to say much to me, and by the time the wedding cake was served the kids were squarely with the program. (Any event that ends with big slabs of cake should not be condemned, in the straightforward ethics system of most children.) Alan and Ryan came up to the frosted creation and posed willingly for photos with their peppy, optimistic dad and some lady in dark gold who would from that point forward, not that anyone had yet spelled this out for them, take on the role of their stepmother.

That was me. The lady in dark gold. And if I had a hard time, in the era of Richard, stepping back into the interior of that person, maybe it's because I kept seeing her as she looked in the photographs; we had them up framed around the condo, the way people do, to remind themselves and anyone who stops by that the couple did get married. (I always thought it a strange tradition, as if without the photographs everyone might forget, but once you're married you find yourself falling into these conventions, like someone helplessly tipped over into a well of cold water.) She, the bride that day, was beautiful, if you want to know, and her rosehip lips were smiling broadly, enough that you could tell she must have had extensive orthodontic work done as a child, and though her makeup was not perfect—it never was, frankly—neither was it in this instance garish or gaudy, and it lent a small extra sparkle to her green elsewhere-directed eyes. The lady in the pictures was elegant, pretty, watching the lean, good-looking man with pleasure, stepping in to a kiss, holding a bouquet of pale flowers. Sure, she looked happy. Forget about Disneyland! This was it. This was the day. This had to be the day of all days.

But how far did it go, that impression? Did it apply to anything other than the moment of that particular photograph, and isn't it true that cameras only tell you so much, namely what a person is holding out for the world to see, with the burnt-gold layers disguising whatever might be inside—the core, the kernel of a different truth altogether?

What was she feeling, really, that bride?

I loved the man I was marrying. That much I can say with a full heart in my throat and the requisite tears in my eyes. He was a punster and a gentleman and a sentimentalist, in a good way, the kind capable of tearing up over underdog sports victories or ads for arthritis medication, those ones where old folks frolic through fields with their grandchildren. I loved and still do love that man who was turning, in the pictures, into my husband. The transfer was occurring. He was becoming, to use that strange, inhuman, and yet deeply human possessive—*mine*. Possession is nine-tenths of the law. Right? Who said that? What was it said about, originally? Husbands? Probably not.

Because, you see, I could not then and never would be able to think of marrying the man I married without thinking of the woman he married before me. Theresa's curse was effective in that regard, spreading its poison across the years. I don't care how many dinners I cooked for the guy, shepherd's pie, pot roasts, fish cakes, roast chicken, I don't care how many launderings I completed of his most personal garments, how many stray nose hairs or fingernail clippings I swept into my palm and the bin, how many of the unspoken intimacies of cohabitation I lived through as his *wife*, goddamnit, it said so on a piece of paper and I had the ring on my finger to prove it—he had still belonged to someone else first. I was not Choice Number One. The plaid living-room set would never let me forget that, and even if she did, there would always be Alan and Ryan to remind me.

I should mention the day of the proposal. The man with the brave arms and favorable mouth, whose words covered me in sweetness, as if he alone were able to absolve me of all manner of sin or mistake—he looked into my eyes in some sticky aftermath moment, minutes after the sweat and grunting that characterize human beings urgently making love. He gazed at me—I think it's appropriate to use the word "gaze," it was a fairytale moment—sort of—and then this man, my lover, said: "Will you marry me?"

The question stopped my breath. I had never been asked, never imagined being asked, like my mother I had given up on any hopes in the matrimonial department. It just hadn't seemed to be in the cards for me. Yet here was this man and he was asking me to marry him. Me! I might become somebody's wife, after all. And not just anybody's—*this* man's, this kind, strong, handsome man's.

When my breath came back, though, it somehow wasn't the above that I expressed—my joy, my surprise, my acceptance. What I actually said was more pragmatic, and risked sounding cool.

"Don't you think—" I said nakedly to the man who would one day become my husband, after the necessary trading of vows and rings at the boathouse down by the bay, "Don't you think it might be best if you got divorced first?"

Pantry of Delights

Statute of Limitations — Unfortunately there is no general consensus on how long bitter, resentful grudges can be held by those who feel they have been abandoned. You may believe there to be a reasonable limit—one year, two years, three years, even—but there has been no clear ruling on the matter.

Furthermore, even if there had been, compliance would be unenforceable.

⟶

Before I met Richard, when I used to stand at the stationery store waiting for customers, I would think about that couple in the photographs. They were everywhere in the condo, I saw them all the time, along with pictures of Alan and Ryan, who grinned against the textured blue school background or in colorful sports uniforms holding some bat or ball or other. Grinning, like: Life is great! The divorce hasn't bothered me one bit! I'm just a cheerful, spunky kid and am ready for your best pitch. Play ball!

And the couple looks so confident. He, particularly, the man with the straight shoulders in the crisp white shirt, seems sure he will be able to carry everyone through. Oh sure, it might be a little rocky for a while, maybe a couple of months or so while domestic complications are ironed out and everyone gets used to the new arrangements, but after that it will be clear sailing: the pair kissing as husband and wife now, legitimately, and the boys making cute TV-sitcom appearances during which they say something winning and then disappear handily from the set. The lady in burnt gold will try out a bright cereal-commercial kind of smile on school mornings as she packs up the boys' lunches (the sandwiches! the pasta salads! the fruit leathers!—oh, is she *ready*), and in the evenings she will help adjudicate their fiercely competitive games of Monopoly or chess. The guy will soldier on, trying to pretend things are swell—*We're getting there, it's fine or soon will be, it very soon will be.*

But in fact. The bed of thorns; the going to bed with dogs and the waking up with fleas; the tossing, restless sleep of the guilty, the cursed, the joint-custody blighted. Accusatory scenes and mad tantrums singing us to our rest. When Theresa had to drop off the children she parked a half-block down from our condo. She would not look at me, she would not talk to me, she would not utter my name. She did her proud best to obliterate me altogether, though she was continually able to draw my husband into the fray, where he followed her, obediently, like a well-trained great Dane. Handover hiccups and Christmas Day confusions, the two parents bartering presidents and heroes as if they were high-level terrorists (if you get Martin Luther King Day shouldn't I get George Washington?). And over it all, money troubles oozing like a constant hot lava, burning our feet and making the room too hot, and not in a good way. The plaid living-room set getting her alimony and her child support, spending it wisely on new Egyptian cotton sheets and swanky outfits for her low-self-esteemed self ("Well, I need to do something for *me*"), letting us pick up the tab for minor expenses like school fees and dental bills. And me, with my youthful adventures in orthodontistry, how could I begrudge those buck-teethed boys that?

Into this pantry of delights walked dear Richard, like a guy looking for a quick handful of snack crackers who happens upon a larder stocked to the ceiling with pickled jalapeños, tins of snails, out-of-date tuna fish, and other unsavories, along with a small mouse in the corner (that's me), squeaking, "Help me! Get me out of here! *Do* something! Please!"

He really wasn't looking, Richard, at the time, for either a mouse or a friend. I'm sure he had plenty of both. His living situation may have been unclear to me, even after we'd struck up an ongoing conversation—it was one of those details about which he managed to be quietly evasive—but it seemed evident from his tales (he liked to tell tales; *likes*, I mean, I may as well use the present tense; the man isn't dead) that people flocked to him often, doubtless drawn, as I was, to his warmth, his red hair, and his size, as well as his easy reflections on the world that got you thinking. I was like a lot of people that way, finding Richard difficult to resist. The man was a honey pot, a soft patch of grass, a wrap of smooth cashmere—he was somewhere people wanted to be.

I couldn't imagine when I would see him again, though, my health-mart fantasies notwithstanding. Far likelier that I'd barge into Mother Theresa by the bread wall or catch sight of her across a dead sea of root vegetables. The proximity of our condo to my husband and DDT's former house of bliss was a sadistic or, more charitably, naive choice on my husband's part, part of his earlier dewy-eyed plan for the two domiciles to get along in Brady-like fashion. (We never did make it to lighthearted sitcom banter about our predicament, sadly. We were all three, rather, following the lines of some dark modernist opera: all atonality and dissonance, and obscure, haunting refrains.)

You can see it a little easier now, can't you? How I was ready to meet a guy with envelopes who talked in broad terms about the universe and its workings? (It didn't have to be envelopes, of course; it could have been Post-Its or pencils.) The universe had been mysterious to me previously but, more to the point, my head had not been high enough for me even to take a look in the universe's direction: my not-so-level gaze was down at the level of car payments and condo fees, and whether it made more sense to blow some cash on a really great vacation or save it toward paying the tuition for the boys' private school, where they were acquiring necessary life skills like how to make PowerPoint presentations on subjects in world geography, and say, "Charge it, please," in various languages.

Before I met Richard, this was how my thinking, such as it was, rattled along while I stood in the stationery store. I reflected on the fact that my husband and I did not make love as frequently any more, urgently or otherwise, and how when we did my mind was often elsewhere, though nowhere very sanitary or illuminated: Don't forget to take out the recycling, and did we still have eggs in the dark recesses of the refrigerator, and why could she, Mother Theresa, not get a job, actually, around the hours of her saintly school volunteering? And *why*—this the question underneath so many of my ant-like complaints and beetling irritations—*why had he married her in the first place?* What did this supposedly discerning man, whose judgment I was meant to trust, in that he had singled me out for love and companionship, see in a dear darling soul who had done little in five years but be vile and vituperative, manipulating said man with her histrionics and demands? He must have loved her once, my husband, and furthermore promised to do so into his dotage, since that is the format of wedding-day oaths, as we know. What had he been thinking? (Oh, she must have been nicer then, of course, her brown helmet hair softer, her queenly demeanor more forgiving, and perhaps under all that armor she even had a sense of humor; though I, invisible as I was, had never been permitted to see it.) If he was capable of such a misstep then, about someone he went ahead and procreated with—twice—you had to ask yourself whether his notion of our great destiny together, that is, his and mine, held any water at all. The man had made a mistake with Theresa; he had said as much to me, often. Was there an unwritten day in our future when he would be murmuring the same about me to another lady altogether, someone new and hopeful who was sharing his bed?

Or was there a day in our future when I would say that about him?

Into this pantry of delights walked Richard, and you have to understand that when Richard came into a fairly small, crammed store like Mr. Finkelstein's, the shelves tended to reverberate and the air became that much closer. He took up a good deal of space. But in retrospect, the space was there, waiting, waiting for someone like Richard—no, for Richard himself, specifically for *Richard*—to come and fill it.

Our first conversation was, as I've said, brief and allusive. Little hint of the philosophy that was to come. But from that first hand clasp across the melamine I had the sensation that this man would stir something within me. Sometimes one small touch is that telling. Before you even know the other person, their votes or their dreams, their eating manners or reading habits, your body has staked out its claim, telling you clearly, *This is someone to meet. To know. To hold.* You start thinking about cooking for them, one day. In my case, that is always a sign.

He came back to the stationery store. The next week. This was unexpected. Ancient Milton only ever used to come by every six months or so; then again, Milton was experienced, the originator of the envelope and the business, and also he was a hundred years old so did not get around easily and was loath to make unnecessary trips. Richard was young and he was fresh and he was pushing the envelope. That—or maybe he liked me.

"Hello!" he called out cheerfully when he came in, the voice of a man in an advertisement. "I'm Richard—the man with the envelopes." As if I wouldn't know! "How's tricks?"

"Tricks are for kids," I said, dredging up some ancient call-and-response cereal commercial from my youth, and though it seemed stupid it made him laugh.

"I remember that one." He chortled. *"Silly rabbit."*

Those pop-culture inanities can, in their way, forge a bond.

"I'd suggest that you sit down, make yourself at home," I said to Richard boldly, as if I already knew him, "but there really isn't room. We run a tight ship, as Mr. Finkelstein likes to say."

"I see that." Richard looked around the well-stocked shelves. "This is a place for people with a purpose. Not so much for distracted dawdling, idle chatting."

"People usually come in here knowing what they want," I affirmed. "They come in with a mission."

"None of the aimless browsing you see in the bookstore or at a clothes shop."

"They come in here to get organized." I was articulating something to Richard I had noticed over the years but had never shaped into words before. "They're trying to put things in order."

"Of course!" His bottle-green eyes fizzed like they'd just been filled with a snazzy new soda. When Richard got hold of an idea he liked, his whole face came to life. "All these files and labels are about putting things in their places."

"Containing the chaos," I said.

"Keeping entropy at bay," he added.

"For a few days, at least. It always comes back. Entropy never stays gone long."

"It's a faithful friend," he said.

"A loyal companion."

"That it is," Richard concluded, and we looked at each other and smiled. It was our first conversational riff. We had fallen easily into a rhythm together, and that's a rarity. We both exhaled, as if we'd been running.

"It's funny," I ventured, again as if we were already weeks into our acquaintance and I was picking up a thread from an earlier exchange—the way you sometimes meet a person you feel you started talking to years before, just somewhere offstage or in your dreams, without anyone knowing—"I've never thought about it quite like that."

"Though you're in here several days a week."

"Monday through Thursday. Friday's my day off." I was telling him something: when he would find me there, if he happened to drop by again.

Mr. Finkelstein emerged from the back just then, reeling a customer along with him. He had been in deep consultation with a lady looking for boilerplate rental forms. You could tell from the way they were talking and shaking their heads that she and Mr. Finkelstein had exchanged words about tenants and their tendencies, the stresses and strains of allowing other human beings to inhabit a piece of property you own. Mr. Finkelstein is skilled in this regard, like a therapist: he reflects back to the customer what he thinks they want to hear. People confess all sorts of things to Mr. Finkelstein. He looks ordinary enough, an older gentleman with serious glasses and a vaguely beaglish expression, but there's a trustworthy air about him that gets people talking.

Richard and I backed up, me so my boss could squeeze through to the cash register, and Richard to allow room for the landlady to pay; except that in doing so his backward step took him crashing into one of the birthday-card stands, which teetered threateningly. He steadied the metal contraption with hands full of fluster, and by the time he turned back to us his round face was artificial-crab-pink with embarrassment. "I'd best be going," he said to me. "I'll see you again, sometime."

"I hope so." I tried not to sound desperate. I then spent the rest of the day diligently noticing all the ways customers who came in were making efforts of containment—that appealing, elusive goal. Though there would always be those who were just after stickers and pens.

It's funny how one small spark, one little light, can change the look of so much. I went home to some familiar entropy of my own: kids' games and insurance bills, scattered CDs and some new burden of forest-depleting catalogues in the mailbox, the very clutter I'd spent much of my day helping other people ward off. On a regular evening like this there would be every chance I'd step over the threshold shuddering with irritation at my husband, whose children were apparently constitutionally incapable of clearing up after themselves—a feature that, to be fair, they seemed to have inherited from their father, who himself allowed me to feed and launder him without any second thought as to whether or not the arrangement was entirely equitable. Who would come back to the condo an hour or two after me, tired and demanding, listing the faults of his co-workers before reaching for the remote control and allowing televised inanities to wash over him, rendering him pliable if numbed.

Normally this all would have bothered me to no end. I knew I hadn't married a modern man who'd wear his kids around his neck in a pouch, but it would have been nice to have the guy familiarize himself with a few basic appliances like the dishwasher and Sudmeister. But that day, buoyed by my jokey exchange with the Irish-seeming Santa Claus, I felt uncharacteristically patient with my husband. I listened to his worries and complaints with new sympathy, happy to sedate him later with his favorite crime show; I dealt with the customary disarray of his personal habits with less lip-biting disgust. (Think *nose hair*, think *clippings*, think *all over the bathroom sink*.)

Our weeks had these strange syncopated rhythms: the lopsided shorter spells packed with taking care of the boys, lunchboxing them, homeworking them, hauling them hither and yon so they could bat and kick balls for sweaty glory, then preventing them from mauling one another once they got home, all while delivering the occasional life lesson, if we could squeeze it in, to offset whatever edicts were handed down by DDT (a program of selfishness and blind loyalty, or that's how it looked to me). Then Cheerios off the table and backpacks out from underfoot and the boys were gone, phew, for another five or six days, my husband and I left alone together again with the reassuring (or poignant, or bewildering) photographs from our wedding, and the right to indulge in bad habits like reading at the table, or eating cheese and breadsticks for dinner, that we would try to avoid when Alan and Ryan were around.

A relief, you might say, to have those stretches in our shared adult destiny together again, without the boys on hand. Yet, when it came to it, those boyless days sometimes carried with them a low drumbeat of dread, the recognition that our shared adult destiny was not the flower-entwined one of the fairytale. It wasn't the one keenly anticipated by the rice-covered people in the wedding pictures. It wasn't even looking like the Grand Passion that could explain the abandonment of the plaid living-room set, odious though she might have been. We were there—there we were—a regular, dissatisfied married pair, each doing our bit for the other (earning money, laundering underwear) but not, as a matter of fact, talking enthusiastically or embracing sincerely or gazing at the other one, frankly, with anything brighter than low-wattage acceptance. My husband's arms were still strong, and he still on some level meant well, but he had forgotten about trying to save

me, so absorbed was he in his own narrative of bitterness and carp-
ing. As for me, the cement under those leaves was proving awfully
damned hard, and I could not seem to find my way to a place that
was softer. The setup was sad, and it was certainly worth denying
or ignoring in order to avoid upset, but that was the state of the
matrimonial state before I met Richard. Once he entered my life, I
felt easier about the gaps with my husband at home. I could wash
dishes all night without cavil, wondering when I would see him
again. The other guy, I mean. Richard.

He came in the following week. Again. To Mr. Finkelstein he
said he was just in the neighborhood, meeting with another
account (probably Smithson's down on University Street, you
could see Mr. Finkelstein's beady mind working, *that* shabby
operation with its dusty, disordered interior, which used its privi-
leged location near the college to overcharge on everything)—
and thought he'd stop by to make sure all was well with us
here, vis-à-vis envelopes. Mr. Finkelstein assessed this comment
correctly as a bit of blather, a smoother-over, but such were
Richard's charms that even Mr. Finkelstein, who was polite and
helpful to all while privately having liking for none, seemed to
breathe more easily, more deeply, in his presence. I swear I saw
my boss shrug, slightly. He knew why Richard had come and he
thought that was fine, bless him, and he said he was going to go
into the back to make some coffee and would either of us like
some? "Sounds great, thank you," Richard nodded like an eager
son-in-law-to-be, and off Mr. Finkelstein tottered to the back
room, the employees-only area that was the dense, circuitboard-
like headquarters of the Finkelstein operation.

"There's a café four doors down," I murmured to Richard, "that sells nice cappuccinos and has a wide selection of teas."

"Let me guess—your boss thinks that's a waste of money? A rip-off?"

" 'For the amount they charge for one of their fancy coffee beverages—' "

" '—I can make twenty perfectly tasty cups right here!' "

I raised my eyebrows. "Have you heard him?" I whispered.

"Just a guess." He grinned. I've never trusted grinning, the action or the word—usually when people *grin* in books they have only two dimensions, they aren't characters you can hold on to—but the fact is, Richard had a short grin in addition to his wider smile. The grin was a kind of telegraph: *I'm with you on this one.* It was a signal, a flare. It made you want to grin back at him, but grinning has never been an art I possess. I have more of a line in the rueful sideways smile or the occasional honest floodlit beam. The expression of real happiness. You don't see that one often.

"I used to have a boss," Richard said, in the same low, confidential tone, "when I was a teenager, in Chicago. I got a job working in a model store—remember when models were a big deal, ships, airplanes? I don't think kids do as many models anymore."

"It's all Lego. Lego products that tie in with big movies. Spaceships, superheroes, kid wizards."

"Right. Well, back then—" How old was Richard? Older than me, I guessed, but there seemed no reason to get specific. "It was models, and I was obsessed with making models, and this job, this Saturday job, was heaven for me because I got to be around them and talk about them—even occasionally build one, for the display window—and all the other kids and adults who came in there were obsessed with models too. We were like a club. We were like a *church*."

I nodded. I could see it. I tried to imagine this big guy shrunk down, a kid, beardless, talking about models. In Chicago, where I had never been.

"Anyway, Mr. Mayer, my boss—I called him Oscar, to myself, because of the hot dogs—he had very strong opinions about not wasting anything. Food, money, time. His motto was *thrift*. And so it drove him wild that though my mother packed me a beautiful sandwich lunch for those Saturdays when I came to work in the store, all I wanted to do on my break was go to the diner around the corner and order a hamburger. That was my idea of freedom: a hamburger at the diner, bought with my own money. That meant I was a person in the world, you know? I had arrived. It drove Mr. Mayer nuts that I wouldn't just sit in the back room with him eating my liverwurst sandwich and pickle. 'Your mother went to all this trouble for you!' he'd yell at me. 'What're you going to do, waste it?' But the point was, I didn't waste it at all. There was a guy who came in on Saturdays, every Saturday, a lonely old bachelor named Mr. Penny, and somehow I found out that Mr. Penny craved nothing more in life than a homemade sandwich—his mother had died a few years earlier, and I guess no one made sandwiches like *she* did, until my mom came along with her liverwursts and her egg salads, which Mr. Penny was perfectly happy to buy off me. So it wasn't a waste at all. The money I made on the sandwich helped pay for my hamburger. And Coke. —Thank you, Mr. Finkelstein. Hot coffee. Delicious."

And Richard winked at me—winking, which is right alongside grinning in my lexicon of clichéd gestures, but again the man was cute, he was good at it—and took the cup from Mr. Finkelstein. To my nose it was a weak, hickory-infused brew, but Richard sipped it appreciatively and cracked a few harmless jokes with Mr. Finkelstein about politics, the latest scandal or debacle, and suddenly there we three were, enjoying our little kaffeeklatsch. Richard told a few more stories, specifically envelope and stationery stories. He made Mr. Finkelstein laugh—a sound you heard only every six months or so—with an account of an account in the suburbs, a brightly colored store in a mall staffed largely by teenaged daughters of the owner, who had an unfortunate tendency to leave traces of lipstick and nail polish on the merchandise they handled, then wonder why people complained. This sketch combined several of the elements Mr. Finkelstein found most provocative—malls, teenaged girls, and stains—and I think his rare bark of laughter had in it the yelp of hysteria.

It felt like Thanksgiving dinner by the time Richard was through. That replete, *Well* that *was delicious!* sensation, as you push back from the table and recline further into the chair—to the extent its stiff right angle makes possible—while searching for a suitable moment in which to emit a subtle burp. (A discretion you wouldn't find in Alan or Ryan, who could never be persuaded it was anything other than riotously funny to have a loud eructation contest brought on by the special-occasion sparkling apple cider we served them with the holiday meal.) Richard emptied his coffee cup, uttered a pleased "Ah!" that was just this side of parody, and then checked his watch as if to square off for all the envelope stops still ahead of him. "I'd really better be going," he said. "I've lingered too long already."

A paralegal-type came in then (young, officious), looking for eight-and-a-half by fourteen file folders, which allowed Mr. Finkelstein to nod and disappear without having to be effusive about it. That left me and Richard.

"I loved hearing your stories," I blurted, though softly, like some dopey thirteen-year-old talking to a pop star.

"There are plenty more of them." Richard lifted an eyebrow. "I didn't even get to the one about the party-preparation store I ran before Milton started to groom me for envelopes."

I smiled at that, but it was the sideways rueful kind, meaning: when would we ever have time to get to party preparation?

"I'll stop by again," Richard said softly. "Maybe one day we could have lunch, even."

I loved that *even*. Like we both had something to hope for. Like he was, for his own part, eager. I nodded shyly and he departed the store quietly, leaving me afloat, hovering, on the warm air of possibility.

Later that day, after a mother had come in and knocked over the sticker rack with the help of her unleashed two-year-old, and after a crabby lady had demanded a refund on a stapler she claimed had malfunctioned, when it merely had an easily cleared staple jam, and after a few other faceless sorts bought birthday cards and tape refills—my husband stopped by. In the late afternoon. Something he hadn't done since the early days, when he still felt romantic, and would come in to make sure I was doing all right in this job he had found for me. He'd buy a dozen pens from the store and, as he put it with jokey lasciviousness, watch my dexterity at the cash register. Ker-ching!

Isn't it a funny thing about people who love you? They have instincts, even when they aren't paying any attention. My husband didn't look at me carefully enough that afternoon to notice that my shoulders weren't as sunk in as they had been before, or that humor and anticipation were now lighting my face; and Mr. Finkelstein, for his part, gave nothing away, greeting my husband with the same morose beaglish expression he normally did, as if he hadn't earlier shared a fine cup of coffee and Thanksgiving dinner with his hypothetical son-in-law. My husband made a subconsciously smart move, stopping by that day to interrupt the fulsomeness of my fantasies about Richard. (Lunch! Where? When? What would we talk about? Might he not accidentally on purpose put his hands over mine again?) But once in the store, my husband failed to make use of the advantage. To be blunt, he blew it. He looked through me, as had been happening so often lately, straight to the source of his latest sore point: his ex-wife and money.

"She sent me this, for Christ's sake," my husband said, putting a torn-open envelope down on the melamine counter, where recently had rested Richard's bulk and his coffee cup.

It was a bill. A plumber's bill, from the other house, the house they used to live in and own together. One of the boys had flung a piece of Lego down the drain and the overpriced callout service had charged her a hundred and fifty bucks to remove it.

"She says she can't swing it this month, and am I willing to cover it, since it's an expense caused by the boys."

"You should talk to your lawyer," I sighed. I felt as though someone had just thrown a chain around my feet, and I was about to fall over.

"I'm going to. Believe me. This is ridiculous. She's gotten completely out of hand." He shook his head, picked the envelope back up. "Though it'll cost me as much to talk to the damned lawyer as it would to just pay the bill for the plumber."

I sighed again, and we stood there, together, looking past one another at other things.

"Well, sweetheart." It was my job to say this. I was a wife, after all. I knew the script. "How about if I come home and cook you something nice for dinner?"

Falafel Joint

Nutrition — Don't go on a strange diet. It looks suspicious.

⌐

Slowly, slowly. The feelings build, the conversation wanders and evolves. Layers are added. Chicago, the mother who loved him, the friend who taught him the trick of opening soda-pop bottles with his teeth, the leaf-raking scam. (With a couple of pals, he raked the leaves off of a couple's lawn, for a small fee, raking them right over onto the lawn of the neighboring house, whose doorbell the boys then rang: "Hello, you seem to have a lot of leaves on your front lawn. Would you like us to rake them up for you?" So on and so on, from one end of the street to the other, collecting their payments. Pocketing enough to fund comic books and candy all round.) Slowly a person, with his quirks and his history, his particular accent—Chicago—his distinctive gestures—a brisk tilt of his head when he reached the punch line of a story—the look of him, the imagined feel of him . . . Slowly this person becomes a part of you. You open your arms and you embrace this new person, allow

him to become familiar. He comes to reside inside of you, taking
up his own niche within you, a home away from home, so that he
is with you even when you don't see him or talk to him. He is simply keeping you company, making you feel better about the grind
and unhappiness of your regular life. He is there, quietly hidden
(even if he is a big man, as he is), and making you feel better. He is
a poultice. A balm.

And this, before you even have lunch!

It took us several more weeks before we could make lunch
work—something to do with the vagaries of Richard's travel
schedule, which was shrouded in mystery. He had a life on the
move, driving all over, I gathered, in a vehicle I imagined to be a
van or a truck but never actually saw. It was curious, with Richard,
how I came to know certain details about him that made him seem
like a brother, someone I'd known my whole life. He told me a
long story once, when Mr. Finkelstein was away from the store at a
one-day stationers' conference, all about his first girlfriend when
he was sixteen who was a trampoline enthusiast, and how the two
sets of parents—his, and hers—were sure these great kids were
going to get married one day, they were so perfect together. He
and the girlfriend even went off and started college at the same
place and shared a house and a dog together. Then Richard left
college suddenly, and left her, and came West, because he felt the
West was where he was meant to be. The universe was drawing
him there. This story baffled me. It seemed to have a few holes in it
(Did the girlfriend bug him? Was he flunking out of school? Why
else leave so abruptly?), but there wasn't time to fill in the details as
I had to help someone find double-sided scotch tape—it was right

there next to the other tapes, as you'd expect, but sometimes customers are children you need to lead by the hand—and by the time I had dealt with that, Richard was elsewhere.

The point is, I knew that sort of thing about Richard—first girlfriend's name (Linda) and appearance (blonde, pretty), how she talked (with gushes of enthusiasm that made it seem as though she was bouncing on a trampoline, even when she wasn't)—but I did not know what kind of car he drove. When I asked him he said, "Yeah, I parked it a few blocks away in a special spot I've found, where I won't get a ticket."As if that were an answer. A car tells you something about someone, whether he pilots a wide old-style American boat or a tidy, reliable Japanese compact, or a beat-up, bumper-stickered Swedish station wagon (we had a lot of those around in our neighborhood, exhorting an end to the current presidency or, more generally, the establishment of world peace).

Maybe Richard was a pickup guy, sitting high in the cab, hauling who knew what around in the back; or maybe he drove one of those generic vehicles like they rent you at airports, models you never hear of again that appear to be made entirely of plastic. Or was he the owner of, God forbid, a van? I mean the ugly, snub-nosed, family-type vans, the kind DDT drove, wearing her martyrdom on her dashboard like a BABY ON BOARD sign: *I'm a mother with a hell of a lot to do, that's why I have to have all this room, to cart around my children and their gear and their friends and my grocery bags.* I'm afraid my husband and I, in one of the lower forms of second-marriage entertainment, had been known to indulge in mockery of Theresa and her van. She only bought it after the divorce—"If she couldn't have me," my husband once said drily with the humor we somehow used to be able to muster about the situation, "she was damn well going to have a van"—and we were, in fact, still helping DDT pay off that van. Another way my husband's deal, in the split, allowed for strange emotionally laden unfairness.

In any case, I did not know what Richard drove. That was one essential thing about him I did not know. Nor did I know where he lived, or how, or with whom. He had made references to a long commute, but when I asked him from where, exactly, he gestured vaguely, perhaps in the direction of the bay, perhaps toward the hills, it was hard to say which. "A small place—over there—one of those little hamlets." (Who, besides Richard, would use the word *hamlet* in relation to anything other than Shakespeare?) "Half an hour on a good day, but when there's traffic, good Lord, it can take an hour or more." In the area where we lived, the dense urbanity of northern California, a patch so appallingly desirable, apparently, that it had become crowded beyond reason or comfort, Richard's phrase could describe dozens of different locations.

I didn't press him for specifics. Standing together in the stationery store over cups of weak Finkelstein joe—our kaffeeklatsch having become a regular weekly happening that autumn, so that whenever Richard stopped by, Mr. Finkelstein would get brewing— I could not bring myself to come right out and ask Richard if he lived with someone or was married, or, in the sexless vernacular, partnered. That would have been too blunt, a billy club of a question, walloping him with my curiosity about his personal circumstances.

A curiosity that, incidentally, he did not seem to share about me. I made a point of dropping the occasional reference to *my husband* into the conversation, like one of those antacid pills that starts bubbling away in the bottom of the glass, but if it made our talk more difficult for Richard to swallow, he didn't show it. I wore my wedding ring, of course, so I suppose the phrase couldn't have surprised him, but I found it odd that he did not nod or inquire. Indifference, you might hiss in my ear, and believe me the thought crossed my mind: I wasn't so blind with affection for my outsized leprechaun that I didn't wonder if this spark, this light between us, might be something only I felt. Perhaps, I reflected, these exchanges were, for Richard, all rather dim, and just tasted of bad coffee. After all, he had dozens of other friends around the place, he had made that clear. Perhaps he was only in our humble stationery store because he liked to tell his stories to an appreciative audience. (The one about the Ferris wheel and the falling hot dog; the one about his sister and him hiding in the museum; the one about the beautiful girl in junior high he had a crush on, who was so nasty to him he took up wrestling in self-defense. He became so good he won second place in a county-wide wrestling tournament half a year later, and still claimed to have a mean half nelson.)

I did notice that Richard rarely asked me any questions. My husband wasn't the only aspect of my life he seemed uninterested in; he never tried to find out where I was from or who my parents were, any of the standard, placing pieces of biographical information. Jobs, homes, friends: he never asked. On the other hand, I acquired that kind of material about him—it accumulated in the buildup from all of his tales, like silt on a riverbank. I knew something of Richard's past geographies, previous employments, his wide network of buddies and acquaintances. He seemed to know people all over. "I was talking to a friend of mine, Bill, the other day, down in Los Angeles. I used to live there too, some years ago . . . " Richard had also lived in Seattle, Sandpoint, Idaho, and Phoenix. He had not always worked in paper products, nor did he necessarily plan to continue, indefinitely, in paper products. When Mr. Finkelstein was out of earshot, clearing a paper jam out of the lone copier or lurking in the back room concocting the particular Finkelstein potion, Richard talked about other possibilities he might one day explore. He was open, as he put it, to interesting propositions: his friend Rex had come up with a terrific fire-extinguishing substance, made from recycled Styrofoam, and together they were talking about applying for a patent; he had an acquaintance named Kelsey who was developing a line of clothing items made from corn fibers, which might have particular use in third-world countries; and he was in touch with some whiz kid in Nebraska who was coming up with a simple, cheap construction brick made out of carbon (slogan: Carbon: It's Nature's Building Block, and It's Ours Too!). To all of this I listened without having to reciprocate with any of my own stories about past romances, dashed career hopes, places I moved to with a sense of adventure, only to return from defeated, tail between my legs.

Certain utterances of mine, though, Richard did seize on, when I allowed my mind to unfold, unfurl, as it used to regularly, before it got gummed up by the plaid living-room set and those lawyers' bills' figures. There was something about conversation with Richard that brought me back to a younger self. Back in the olden days, troubled and solitary though I may have been much of the time, I did have a mind that liked to look at large patterns, to move in broad sweeps. I wasn't so caught up then in divided loyalties and Cheerios, school runs and condo payments. When I crossed a bridge over water I would tend not to think, What date was this built? Is it the longest or the widest? What is its load, its engineering, its history?—all of these being the sorts of questions my husband excels at asking, and answering. Rather, I'd think something more awed and primitive. You know: Look at the faith we have collectively, driving along here, that this strip of concrete and metal will keep us from falling into the watery abyss. Isn't it funny how determined man is to cross bodies of water, rather than just waving at the other shore from here and leaving them to it. How impossible living around this bay would be if it weren't for the bridges, which are miraculous, touched by God, even, if you believe in that kind of thing, though in the mouths of commuters the contructs become merely curses. *Backup on the fucking bridge again. God damn it.* The bridges can begin to seem like mere impediments to arrival in the great golden-gated city, rather than the astonishing vaults of optimism and opportunity that they are.

I said something like this to Richard once. Before we had lunch. And he loved it. I was shy and mumbly, my default delivery, but he coaxed the words and thoughts out of me like a patient piano teacher listening to someone mangle a short piece, but letting the pupil play it again and again till the notes are pure, glorious and perfect. By the end of that particular conversation about bridges, God, and water, I felt Richard and I had entered new territory together, and in fact it was as he left that day that he said, "So— lunch next week. What do you like to eat? What's close?" And all I could think of to say was "Falafel!" which made him say, "Bless you!" and give me one of his grins. "Falafel next week, then. Don't miss it." "I won't," I told him, skipping the part about how between now and then I'd be doing nothing more than counting the minutes. And looking after my husband and stepsons, with a new strain of patience and light in my voice.

It was called the Promised Land, our local falafel joint, which encouraged the people who dined there to feel briefly like the chosen people, whatever their own faith happened to be. It was small and crowded and intense in there, but they never hurried you through a meal or an exchange of ideas. They understood that talking was important and took time. The main lady who worked in the Promised Land, the owner or manager, had short dark hair and grimaced when she took your order, never writing anything down, but once she got to know you, the grimace was tempered with a tiny smile at the edges, and then you felt favored. Chosen among the chosen.

Lunch—this lunch—was the turning point between Richard and me. Lunch is not dinner, nor is it a movie or a dance floor; nonetheless, it is distinct from standing over coffee and chatting. (Lunch was, too, the first step my husband took with me, back when he was just a guy with a cappuccino and a coupla kids and an ever-so-near-to-ex-wife; together we slid down the slippery slope, quickly, from lunch to movie to dinner to dancing. The rest, as they say, is history.) At a lunch you breathe differently. You look at each other with changed eyes. It was a relief to see Richard framed by something other than greeting cards and calendars; the posters of the Dead Sea and the Wailing Wall made an evocative background. It was like seeing someone out of uniform, the white-coated doctor who performs intimate examinations glimpsed out on the street, in black jeans and boots, transformed from professional to regular, chic person, or the barista at the café spotted later, grounds-free, in the salon getting a haircut. Richard was not, then, the envelope guy. He was a guy with a full beard and field-green eyes, a soft, round face and a voice that soothed and entertained, both. He was a guy I wanted to be around. A guy I wanted to talk to.

At lunch, over glasses of cool minted lemonade and foods salted with sesame, Richard did ask me something. With luck, or with a canniness born of our being kindred spirits, he asked me a question that got straight to the heart of things. "What did you do before turning to the sale of notebooks, envelopes, and pens to the public?"

"Coincidentally enough," I told him, "I *wrote* in a notebook."

"Really? What did you write?"

And rather than the usual dismissal I had trotted out to other strangers over the years—*It was nothing, just rambling, really a kind of glorified diary*—I answered him truthfully. Because he was Richard.

"A Dictionary of Betrayal," I enunciated in a clear voice. "That's what I called it."

"Wow." Richard stopped eating his falafel. He put down his pita bread. "And that's what you were writing? A dictionary, a whole dictionary?"

"Well, I wrote entries, you know, for the different words. Abandonment, cheating, neglect, untruth. Each one had an entry, a story."

"How incredible." He considered for a moment. "And do you have it? Can people read it?"

People. That was endearing. As if Richard was "people"!

"I never finished it." I shook my head. "I only got halfway through."

"Then what? The siren call of the glue sticks and desk planners distracted you?"

I smiled. The shy, sideways kind. "Sort of." But here again I made a decision to tell him, to keep talking. I'd never spelled this out for anyone before. Nobody cared, frankly. "Actually, my husband urged me to give it up. And to get the job at the stationery store."

"Why was that?" He resumed eating after the word "husband."

"He thought working on my dictionary was making me too sad, pushing me inside myself." You have to be fair, when you give these accounts. You can't make people demons.

"Was he right?"

"Probably. It was pretty dark in there. Inside." I remembered the feel of that time with a shudder. All that mourning and difficulty. The dwelling in the dimness of what had already passed. "He thought I was depressed. I probably was depressed. So he thought I should put it away as it just inspired unhappy thoughts. That it would be better for me to have some activity that got me out into the world with other people. It wasn't so much for the extra money, at the beginning, though now with all the incidental expenses of the children and everything the supplemental cash comes in handy."

"You have kids?" Richard asked steadily, and when I said, "Stepkids," he nodded, paused, wiped his mouth, sat up straighter.

"Ah. *Stepkids*," he concurred, as if I had made a profound remark.

"Kids of the step." His eyes wandered off into their fields of green, and I asked my billy club of a question, finally.

"Do you have stepchildren too?" Maybe this explained our connection: we both had that in/out relation to parenthood, when you never know whether you're coming or going. Neither with child, nor child-free. The gray zone. The no man's land.

"I have a stepdaughter. She's grown now, though. Twenty, in college. She's called Sarah." His voice warmed, his eyes brightened, the same look I'd noticed when an interesting idea got hold of him. "She's a peach."

And her mother? Was I allowed to ask? His eyes flickered over to me, anticipating, understanding.

"Sarah's mother and I were married for a few years, a long time ago. She worked at a bakery I liked to go to, which sold some of the world's great scones, sublime morning buns. Best-smelling place on earth. They had bread in the shape of dragons and dinosaurs in the display window, and one day when I went in there was this tiny little serious-faced girl sitting on a stool behind the counter, watching those dinosaurs and dragons as if she was waiting for them to come alive.

"So I see the same pretty girl—I mean, woman, you know, but she was young, she'd always seemed like a girl to me—selling the scones as usual, but her face is all tensed up, all tight. She keeps looking over to the kid and saying, 'Don't touch them, Sarah. Remember what we talked about? You can look, but you can't touch.' And then she turns to me with her regular countertop smile. She had a great smile, like you do, and she says, 'Sorry. Can I help you?' And when I say, 'I see you've got your assistant helping you today,' she tells me that the kid's daycare is closed, the kids have been passing strep around, and the woman who owned the place got it and so the daycare is closed that day, leaving her stranded. 'What a nightmare,' she says, and I can see how stressed she is, so I tell her I don't have to be anywhere for a while and if she likes, I have a pen and some paper, and I could entertain the kid for a while in the back, we could draw some pictures, and she looks so grateful, and we agree that that morning my scones are going to be on the house."

"And from there . . ."

He nodded. "And from there," he agreed, but then stopped, as if that were enough said. "I loved that kid, though. I wanted to look after her. And I felt sorry for Tracy, her mom, having a child so young. She didn't seem ready."

"So you wanted to help her."

"Her and Sarah both. I did love that kid, she was a great kid. Honestly, if it weren't for Sarah I probably wouldn't have dated Tracy. Let alone married her."

"Those efforts to save people, though," I said, taking a sip from my mint lemonade. The drink is one of the Promised Land's specialties: tall, cool yellow glasses speckled with green. "They usually go wrong, in the end."

"You think so?" Richard sat back to consider. "But if you didn't get those urges—if you never acted on those urges—you wouldn't bring people into your life, and then where would you be? I believe when someone makes you feel that way, you've got to act on it. Wherever it takes you. The universe doesn't make mistakes. People come into your life for a reason, even if it doesn't all work out perfectly."

"You don't think the universe makes mistakes?" I asked. This struck me as a fascinating and, I must admit, freakish view. It made me adore Richard more, though, if anything. *You crazy leprechaun. Do you really believe that?* "What about people? Do people make mistakes?"

"When they don't pay attention to what the universe is telling them." This, too, impressed me: did the man have a direct line to the intentions of the cosmos? No wonder he had so many friends. "Listen," Richard said, "if I hadn't dated Tracy, and married her, I'd never have known Sarah. Sarah's one of the best things that ever happened to me. I love that kid. I'm telling you, she's a peach."

"You're still in touch?"

"Oh, sure, of course! She's doing great things at college, she's a junior, she's studying languages and, I don't know, she's going to end up in the global economy somehow. She's terrific. She writes me, I write her, we talk."

"And Tracy?" I pressed.

He shrugged, and lifted his hands in a chosen-people kind of gesture, an apparent indication of defeat. "Well." He sighed. "Like I said, not everything works out perfectly."

Maybe not, but what I gleaned from this exchange did reassure me. Richard had been married. This added real flesh to the portrait I had so far of him, which was still missing key details. (The car. The living arrangements. The voting record.) It filled him out significantly—and it was also a relief. Richard had been married. He wasn't off the grid, relationally speaking. I don't know, you meet a man in his forties who is reasonable-looking and unattached and you wonder, don't you? How off-kilter is this guy? What is the story here? Is he gay, or gay but in denial, or a lifelong bachelor, but I thought they didn't make bachelors anymore, since we all realized that was just code for being a gay man? There's an age you get to where if you haven't managed yet to marry, at least once, it looks pretty suspicious. (I was awfully close to that age myself when my husband came into the café for his cappuccino and found me scribbling away at my shadowy Dictionary of Betrayal. My husband, in marrying me, saved me from having a love life off the grid. I should have been grateful to him for that, no matter the rest of the nightmare. And I was. I was grateful. Forget the Cheerios and lawyers' bills. I was grateful!)

"Why are you so gloomy about people trying to save one another?" Richard turned the tahini-flecked tables now to ask me, and I was glad he did, because it was painful to see even that buoyant man sag under the memory of whatever had gone wrong with Tracy. He had found a way to scoop hope and promise out of the story—Sarah, what a great kid!—but the Tracy part of the episode had not been so peachy, it was clear, and I hated to see the big guy deflated. Let's go back to me and my disasters instead. That was always more comfortable.

So I told him. I told him my story, the fact that I was lonely and odd when my husband discovered me (this was Richard—I could tell him anything, nothing would daunt him, be too much for him; his open face made that clear) and that my husband fell in love with me and rescued me, took me away from my sad dictionary and married me, gave me new life. (If I edged discreetly around the specifics of the hot sloppy kisses, that was in part because there we were, eating falafel in broad daylight, and such references seemed inappropriate; and it may also have been because somewhere my imagination was already reaching toward the image of my kissing *him*, kissing Richard.) I even mentioned that I, in my way, was trying to save him, too—my husband that is—from his unhappy husbandry with Theresa. That I was also trying to give him new life.

"So, that's good," Richard said. "You wanted to help each other. Save one another. What's wrong with that?"

Well! *Here's what's wrong.* So then I had to present a version of the events, considerably condensed or we'd have closed the joint down and I'd never have gotten back to work, that my husband had had to divorce Theresa for this handy rescue to take place, and that divorce was no picnic, as I was sure Richard knew, and this particular divorce happened not just to be no picnic but turned out to be in fact a bloodbath, a catastrophe, a Wailing Wall and a Dead Sea; it was every bad landscape and war metaphor you could come up with, rolled into a two-to-three-year stint of mediation sessions and legal feuds, all of which finally yielded the scenario we were then in: joint custody of Alan and Ryan, and lawyers' bills, money strains, bitterness, and grief.

"Sounds tough." Richard's pale face looked thoughtful over his empty plate. "But the good part is—" And for a minute I worried that this Richard I was becoming infatuated with was nothing more than a Pollyanna, actually, all dressed up in a not-quite-fitting suit and a red beard. "The good part is, you're still together. And you've got the kids—the stepkids. Boys you said, right? So that's some compensation for all the rest."

Compensation! Don't get me started. So then I had to explain what I have already had the opportunity to mention here—that is, that Alan and Ryan did not exactly tug at my heartstrings, that I hadn't quite come to terms fully with the catapults, the computer games, the fart jokes, the Cheerios.

"Oh—they're just being boys." Richard's face was bright again. He had let go of Tracy. "That's what boys do, they can't help it, you just ignore all that to get to the good stuff."

I shrug-nodded noncommittally. Much as I liked this man, he wasn't going to jolly me so easily on the subject of Alan and Ryan.

"Boys are fun to play games with," he continued. "You play games with them?"

"Monopoly."

"There you go."

"We get to become millionaires and bankrupt one another. It's cathartic."

"*Cards,*" he insisted, ignoring this last. Richard was not a great one for sarcasm. "Cards are great—how old did you say they are?"

"Ten and twelve."

"Perfect. Teach them poker. That's a great age for poker."

I was about to shrug-nod again, showing a hint of petulance, but Richard's remark reminded me of something. It reminded me of the hours I spent as a kid playing gin rummy with our old neighbor Millie, back when we lived in the shadow of the mountain. How much I loved those hours. How much I loved her. She had made so much bearable.

"Have fun with them," Richard continued. "They sound like great kids. They're lucky to have you. Think what you can show them, what you can teach them."

"They're very attached to their mother."

"Of course they are." But he said it sympathetically, with the kind of tone Richard could miraculously manage, one of universal sympathy—toward me, dealing with these kids; toward these kids, dealing with me; who knows, maybe even toward DDT herself, the clunky, unwanted plaid living-room set.

"They don't listen to me. I don't think they like me much."

"Don't be ridiculous. Who could help loving you?" He beamed at me, and I paused the moment there, just for a second, like you can on a video or DVD, to watch the two of us, Richard and me, a married lady and the envelope guy, sitting at this falafel joint together, talking. Over the stilled image I whispered the questions to myself: Was this flirting? What was this? Here was this man who emitted a warmth like a heat lamp at a cold outdoor restaurant, a quality I wanted to be around, and here he was saying nice things, flattering things, about me, which brought out the rosehip on my lips and the blush on my neck. But we were talking about my *step-sons*. We were talking about my *husband*. The man was giving me advice on my family, such as it was. Was that flirting?

I wasn't sure of the answer, but never mind. Resume play.

"I just don't think—" I started, pinkly.

"Listen. What's the older one called? The twelve-year-old?"

"Alan." He was the one with the darker brow and the longer nose and the more determined freckles. I pretended I couldn't tell them apart, but of course I could. Ryan was shorter, paler, and thinner, as if the toner had started to run out by the time they got to him and they weren't able to make a really clear copy.

"What's Alan like?"

This was an interesting exercise. I fought off the words *bratty*, *spoiled, mouthy*; the phrase *incapable of picking up his own socks, let alone underwear*. I didn't want Richard to think I was a monster.

"Cocky," I said. "Funny, bossy, swaggery. But—smart. Likes geography and history. Knows a surprising amount about World War II."

"Sounds like the older brother." Richard, I had worked out from the family tales he had told, was the youngest of three. "And the other one? The kid brother?"

Whiny, recalcitrant, moody, morose. "Ryan is soulful. A reader." I struggled. "Hard to engage, in his own world a lot of the time, but if you ever get him to focus on you and what you're saying, and sustain eye contact—you can have a pretty interesting conversation with him."

"There!" Richard sat back, satisfied, as if by a job well done. "You see?"

"What?"

I don't know what it is, or was, with Richard (not that he died, or anything; he didn't). I wanted to shake him, I wanted to hug him, I wanted to give him a big kiss. He seemed so definite about everything. I wanted him to take over. I was making such a hash of things on my own. Maybe he and the universe could sort it all out for me. After all, he did have that direct line.

"Have fun with them. They'll love you. Who wouldn't? You're an angel." And he cupped my cheek ever so briefly in his palm, a touch that lasted shorter than the pulse of a butterfly wing, and was almost as light. The gesture was over before I had a chance even to register it, but the sensation stayed on: the felt imprint, for days, of this man who cared. "That's what I'm going to call you," Richard said in a low voice, under the sounds of the falafel balls frying, the wedges of pita bread toasting. Only I could hear him, now. "*Angel*. My angel."

Angel. His angel.

His.

I soared.

Park Bench

Denial — Don't overestimate the powers of denial. "Of course I didn't—" "Do you really think I would—" "It never happened"—are entirely ineffectual in the face of a jealous spouse.

This is especially true if the denials are false.

—◆—

And where was my husband in all of this? And what was I thinking?

My husband was barking at meter maids. ("Those fascists! Who do they think they are?") He was gnashing his teeth in his sleep. He was shouting at the president on television. ("You're a liar! Go home!") He was hearing rumors at work about cutbacks and layoffs, and each day when he got home he went out to the mailbox like a person heading off into the rioting streets, with a flashlight and a club in hand, expecting a mugging. And with crushing regularity, right after his company posted some jolliness about low third-quarter earnings, DDT would forward my husband some new bill or query. She preferred the paper trail to the modern convenience of e-mail, perhaps thinking that if she physically removed the bills from her own house she could not be responsible for paying them, and so as often as not our mail pickup would be followed by some tense cell-phone exchange during which my husband flailed and hollered. He had programmed Theresa's ringtone on his phone to sound like the sinister snippet from Beethoven's Fifth, which had once seemed quite funny but now just seemed unremarkably apt. (Poor Beethoven. Thank God no one told him the uses his work would be put to, long after his death.)

With the boys my husband was ill-timed and unfocused. He could not remember practice hours or game schedules—the tyranny of organized sports: even as part-timers we were enslaved—so that became my department, along with Homework Check, Lunch Line (the sandwiches! the pasta salads!), Wash and Fold Services, and running the School of Manners. ("Please don't slurp. Because it's unpleasant to listen to, that's why. They may very well allow slurping in Japan, and when you go live in Japan you can slurp all you want, but here at our table I am asking you not to slurp. Thank you.") My husband would stare at his spaghetti and meatballs, at his lamb stew, at his stir-fried chicken and broccoli, and his thoughts would clearly be elsewhere. My best guess was that he was quietly elaborating homicidal fantasies, weighing the risks of ending up on death row against the reward of ridding himself once and for all of the plaid living-room set and her torments, or per- haps of his smug, oily boss. At intervals my husband would look up, try to sharpen his gaze, and say something like, "So how's the science project going?" to Alan, who had just finished describing his experiments with miniature explosive devices, which the three of us had figured would be disallowed. Or, "Hey, Sport. How's soc- cer?" to Ryan, who was fresh from making some surprising, sweet confession that at this point he was only playing because his friend Josh was, and he'd be just as happy to drop it and attend chess club instead.

And me. How was my husband with me? How were we together? Sometimes I was, for my husband, the burr in his sock:
standing near him when he sat at the computer, trying to hover an
answer out of him about some domestic necessity, when all he
wanted was to be left alone watching the satirical news show that
pilloried the government, or some idler's video snippet about his
comical pet. Sometimes I was my husband's sounding board, his
jury, whose job was not to respond or comment but simply listen
and nod as he built his infuriated Shakespearian case against
Theresa. "I don't know what she expects me to do here. I've given
everything. She's bled me dry. What does she want—a pound of
flesh? Is that what she wants?" And sometimes I was simply my
husband's furniture at night, the cushion for his exhaustion or his
anger, the body next to his that he could throw himself at, or into,
when the darkness finally came with its merciful capacity to erase,
and he could wipe out his mind by making love to me, briefly,
before sleep. I let my husband have me, because that's what wives
do, isn't it? It's in the job description. But I was often, myself, not
present when the conjugal conjoining actually happened. I
allowed my husband's familiar form to combine with mine, and I
took part in the appropriate actions of mouth, hands, and hips,
while my mind wandered ever more freely into the happier territory of Richard. And it occurred to me, in those quiet minutes
when my husband had fallen into post-coital oblivion and the
heavy snores were starting, that if I ever started on my Dictionary
again—as I had lately been thinking of doing—there would have
to be a new entry: on imagining one man while making love with
another. This was a category even I, with my various dim experi-
ences, had never considered before.

I was not able to help my husband, and he was not able to help me, and that, I suppose, betrayal or no betrayal, Richard or no Richard, is a sad point to reach in a marriage, when you are both sinking into the murk and neither is able to pull the other one out. If you manage to touch the other, even, to grab at your spouse as you flail, it only has the effect of bringing him or her down with you. I could not ensure my husband's job security, which was wavery, or stop Theresa's rather clever campaign of constant, low-grade morale crushing and money leeching, which had gradually (it took years) transformed my husband from a kind, strong-armed optimist into a foul-mouthed cliché who distrusted the world and its agents (meter maids, co-workers, customer-service representatives). Increasingly he found solace in the bright light of a screen, whether television or computer, though those illuminated squares too were like drugs or alcohol, in that when the immediate palliative effect wore off he was just as grouchy as before, if not grouchier. When I thought of the man I married, pictured in various frames around the condo smiling into the future, and then of this sullen individual I cooked for these days, who tried to but could not escape his carapace of rageful unhappiness—I could only wonder at DDT's power. She began to seem like one of those evil masterminds in a spy movie, controlling events from her secret lair with the operation of hidden switches and devices. My husband had not told me, ahead of time, how canny Theresa was; all he had mentioned was that she alternately nagged and neglected him. I began to wonder whether she was working in legion with the CEO of my husband's company, waging a steady, stealthy assault on my husband's peace of mind. Relentless.

"Don't let them get to you," I tried saying, and, "You can't let her get to you," which was like handing a flyswatter to someone being attacked by a black cloud of locusts. I had never understood my husband's job very well, but I was willing to believe in his narrative of backstabbing office mates and the gathering chill of the approaching "restructuring," and I could not work out how to talk him out of his billowing paranoia and anxiety. As for the plaid living-room set: well, I had never hoped to live with the daily instantiations of her ongoing attachment in the form of the harassing notes and phone calls. You had to feel for the two children (even if they drained you), who were the foot soldiers of the divorce wars, mercenaries drafted in to fight for one side or the other, albeit unwittingly. (Or, in the case of Alan, I sometimes suspected, with complicity. "Mom says the brakes are going on the car and that you took out a repair warranty on it. Do you have it? She says she can feel them grinding every time we pull up to a stop sign.")

All this after five years. Five years! No wonder we weren't as pretty anymore as the people in the pictures. (My husband, once pleasingly lean, was becoming hard-edged and bony; and as for me, I had new lines on my face every morning, permanently etching in my crabbiness and distress.) If you had told that couple, as you scattered rice over them and they blinked and beamed in the celebratory shower, *It's going to be just as bitter in five years as it is right now, I hate to tell you this, and you'll become worn down and gray with it*— they surely would not have believed you. They would not have gone to all that trouble—the flowers, the champagne, the catering and seating charts—if they had not succumbed to the great American banner faith of optimism. We are heading toward a brighter tomorrow! It will all be all right, after a while. A short rocky spell, during the transition, then things will settle down, we'll all be newly happy. *You'll see.*

Every now and then, once the beleaguered man lying next to me was into his slow, rasping breaths of deep sleep, I performed a heretical thought experiment, like the ones they used to give in philosophy class (there are three people in a boat, and the boat will sink unless you toss someone overboard; how do you choose who it should be?). I tried to imagine what that same couple would have said if you had caught them a little earlier—before the rice shower was thrown, let's say, before the vows were vowed, before signatures and destinies were joined in hard print, on the record. If you'd sketched out what was ahead of them—the years of bad-mouthing and slammed-down receivers, the developing dread caused by Beethoven's Fifth tinkled out on the cell phone, the itchy, scratchy concern that the unending conflict was not optimal for the mental health of the children—would either have chosen to call it off? Refused the nuptials after all?

Runaway bride, or gone-for-good groom? *No, hold it, stop, I've changed my mind. Hold up here! Whoa, boys!*

He wouldn't have. The kind, clean-shaven man would have carried on with the ceremony, I'm pretty sure. He would not have carried on with DDT any longer anyway (on that point I had remained convinced), and he loved the rosehip-lipped girl and wanted her, whatever the obstacles. But the sideways-smiling one—what about her? Would she have signed up to richer and poorer, and from this day forward, had she known of the second-wife nausea that would afflict her through the following years? If she had snatched a glimpse of the pantry of delights that awaited her? Or had an inkling of the aesthetic and spiritual effect of having the plaid living-room set in her own living room day after day, taking up space, unattractive, insistent, immoveable?

Would she, reader, have married him?

Rather than answer that question for myself, I chose to think about Richard.

This was such a funner way for a troubled mind to spend its time. I knew myself well, for better or worse (in sickness and in health), and was all too familiar with the small-hours-of-the-morning madness I could descend into, the one-to-four A.M. slot, when my thoughts spun round and round like clothes in the damned washing machine, the difference being that my thoughts in the spinning never seemed to get any cleaner. They just rotated endlessly in agitation, while the subjects they touched on got darker and darker. (This was the state I had been in, too, when penning my Dictionary of Betrayal.) I could spend hours in imaginary supine struggle with Mother Theresa, for instance, asking her who she thought she was helping, dragging us all down this way. (Did she never want to put her boys' peace of mind slightly higher than her own need for attention?) Then again, sometimes, flat on my back in the dark, I marched over to the financial-consulting company that employed my husband, and shouted at the faceless man running it: Don't you see what my husband has done for you? Can't you give the guy a break, stop teasing and tormenting him with hints of his forthcoming severance? Who are you, God, to control people's fate in this sadistic way? Finally, on some black nights, when my chapped hands were tired of wringing one another and my patience had expired entirely, it was often the man lying next to me I fought with, unbeknownst to him, as he dreamed snoringly on. Why can't you help me more? Why didn't you mention, when you proposed to me, that I was going to end up spending so many hours scrubbing and tidying, shopping and cooking? What ever happened to equality in the workplace? Wasn't there a whole social movement somewhere along the line—can't remember the name of it but I have a vague memory of bras near a bonfire—that addressed precisely this issue? Who led you to think I would actually enjoy picking up floor-stuck Cheerios deposited by your adorable offspring?

Why did you tell me to stop writing my Dictionary?

How could I ever have imagined how bad-tempered you would become? Why do you watch so much bad television, and do you suppose it improves my opinion of you or has that ceased to matter? What is the deal with men being unable to turn and face you when you talk to them if there is a lit screen within twenty feet of their eyeballs? When was it exactly (I didn't notice) that your touch became perfunctory, and what happened to all those back rubs I was promised in the cheerier days of our courtship? How could you so blithely have assured me that your marriage to Theresa was all but over? How could you so blithely have assured me that your marriage to Theresa was all but over?

How could you so blithely have assured me that your marriage to Theresa was all but over?

Or, you see, I could think about Richard. Richard was light, he was warmth, he made me laugh. With his straightforward Midwesternness he reminded me of someone I'd loved in the first part

of my life, our old neighbor friend Millie, who came from Min-
nesota and was to ice-skating what Richard was to envelopes. She
had died some time before all this, and I missed her still, and
thought about her often, and these thoughts were circular: recalling Millie's jokes and her notions, above all her gift for affection,
led me right back to thoughts about Richard.

Richard and I had settled into the routine of his coming by the
store once a week. After a cup of Mr. Finkelstein's fine elixir and a
few amusing stationery anecdotes culled from the years, it was
somehow accepted that Richard and I would have lunch together
down at the Promised Land. Mr. Finkelstein was, as far as one
could tell anything about the man in his taciturnity, an upstanding
citizen who applauded fidelity in marriage, yet he never seemed
worried about my lunching with Richard. In fact, it seemed clear
he endorsed it. You sometimes had the feeling he was shooing us
out the door with old-fashioned encouragement: "Go ahead, you
young people, go have some fun at the soda fountain together"—
not that Richard was especially young and nor was I, but around
Mr. Finkelstein it was possible to feel youthful. Mr. Finkelstein
liked Richard and he liked us being together. I think what he saw,
this boss of mine who had known me for several years now, standing by my side as I sold the world manila folders and address
labels, was that I was happier around Richard. I stood taller. I
opened my eyes wider. I breathed, in the sense of taking in the air
and the atmosphere, rather than in the simpler sense of staying
oxygenated and alive.

Richard made me curious again, something I had not even
noticed I was not anymore. Not about politics or the news—as I

said, I still didn't know how he voted, or to what extent he shared our common contempt for the president, since all Richard dispensed on such subjects were one-liners and jokes. He made me interested again in the deeper, truer fabric of life. He talked in a sideways fashion of Zen, which was one of those short syllables I'd heard bandied about but never spent much time with myself. "No one has to be angry about anything: you *choose* to be angry. It's a choice," he said once, when I made a passing reference to Theresa, and I thought, "How fascinating. Can that possibly be true?" Or: "One day they'll find life on Mars. I'm certain of it." I looked into the night sky differently, weighing his opinion. He liked to tell me stories from his past, like the one about the girlfriend he had who was a schoolteacher and kept cats. The cats loved Richard first, until the woman finally took the cue from the two tabbies and allowed him into her bed, where, he implied, very pleasurable things had happened. From this he drew one of his Richardish conclusions on the nature of the world. "Animals feel a vibration before humans do. Did you ever notice that? They can feel earthquakes coming and will start to act jumpy, or the hair goes up on the back of their necks if there's a spirit in the house, and they know if their owners, these human beings they love, are happy around someone. They can just feel it, they don't complicate everything with words and judgments the way we do. You know, 'Yes, but does he make enough money for you?' or 'Is he from the right background?' Animals just *feel* it. Let's say you have a pet you're close to, that pet can communicate to you how you really feel about someone, without this overlay of unimportant surface details. Everyone should have a pet, for that reason." He was quite serious about this, though he sensed, perhaps, the impracticalities for some. "To tell them what they really think."

It was another day at the Promised Land when Richard delivered this speech, and as I chewed my pita bread and tahini I enjoyed the idea of each person having his or her private Chihuahua or Siamese that could dispense wordless romantic advice. Could a dachshund, at this point, have made things different between my husband and me? A Saint Bernard? "If Sally," Richard continued, "my old black Lab, were still alive, for instance, she'd come right over to you and put her nose in your palm, wagging her tail, because she could tell that I adore you. And she'd love you, too."

There it was. I blushed, as I always did when Richard made a remark of that kind. I stopped eating, and felt a hot flush of guilt and excitement. But Richard did not pause over the moment, expanding it or making it more meaningful. He simply carried on, now into stories about wonderful Sally his old black Lab, her adventures and misadventures, as though he had just said something that was fairly obvious already, about adoring me, and there was no reason for anyone to get excited or pay particular attention. ("One two three four five six seven eight nine ten, who's excited? I'm not excited!" This had been one of Millie's steadying refrains.) Richard's love was just something people knew about, one of the solidities of the world, like the fact that Labradors have great hearts but can sometimes be too fetch-obsessed for their own good.

But *I adore you*: he said it, and he called me his Angel, and somehow from his demeanor, even when he was talking to me about my husband, or about Alan and Ryan, it was clear that he loved me.

And love given to you like that, so freely, earns itself back right away; so that although I did not say it aloud, I knew that I loved him, too. I did. I loved Richard, too.

It was like a secret corset I wore, this love, wrapped around my waist keeping me safe and contained. I knew that Richard loved me and I knew that I loved Richard, but like him I wasn't going to overdramatize it, I wasn't going to get all hot under the collar, and I wasn't going to assume it meant anything cataclysmic. My mind became a numb blankness when it got anywhere near the idea of actually leaving my husband, or shedding Alan and Ryan or, for that matter, Theresa. (We were all so *connected*.) I did not explore the future implications of my love for the big guy with the envelopes, I just kept the substance with me, a hip flask in my pocket, to swerve into different metaphorical territory here—a flask I could swig from deeply in the various nightly moments when I needed a hit of something pleasurable to help deal with the boys fighting over their computer games or a husband sitting in front of the news and snarling disgust at the latest White House shenanigans.

And there is something else to say about this love, and the man who called me his Angel. And this something else was why I held on to my flimsy balsawood airplane of self-defense (which would have broken on its very first flight, doubtless, as those crummy things tend to do, had I tried to launch it)—that my friendship with Richard was innocent and unthreatening. The fact is, amidst Richard's declarations of adoration, scattered here or there like the notes he had started to write me, there was scarcely any mention of my physical self beyond the simple and asexual "cute," which as we know can cover anything from puppies in a pet-shop window to a model's skimpy bikini. He was quite careful, my Santa Claus, not to make any sort of references to kisses or bodies, so all there was to go on was the big bear embrace he always gave me when he left after lunch, which was, frankly, indistinguishable from the kind you'd get from your father (if you had one). Richard winked at me, he cupped my cheek in his palm more than once, he occasionally stroked my hair, briefly; he made infrequent references, in passing, to the fact that I was pretty. (Just that, just *pretty*, nothing outsized like *beautiful* or *ravishing*, which I had once been to my husband.) Did Richard love me as a brother? Or an uncle? It seemed possible. Was *Angel* a relative, after all, of *Peach*, the kind of name you give to the little girl you've found wandering around the fairground who has managed to get separated from her parents, with whom you'll make every effort to reunite her? The girl you meet at the bakery, being told she can look but not touch?

Maybe. I couldn't tell, and I couldn't ask him. I could talk to Richard about anything, he made it clear he would listen to me on any subject at all (and that in itself is a gift: someone opening their ears for you, allowing, awaiting the pour), but mumbly as I was, there were things I felt shy about, and the subject of attraction was certainly one of them. What would I have said? I notice everything about you when we eat lunch together, Richard, whether it's the way the pale hair gathers on your thick fingers like a young crop of wheat; or the movement of your wide shoulders under the suit that constricts them; or the undergrowth on your cheeks and chin, that thick, graying fox-bristle I imagine delightfully chafing my face if I ever leaned forward to kiss you. (Though I may never kiss you.)

Will I one day feel you holding me in anything other than an uncle-ish embrace? Will you ever make yourself part of me as I sometimes, at three and four in the morning, illicitly imagine? Will I touch any skin of yours other than that of your hands?

He started to write me notes. Richard carried three-by-five index cards around with him in his inside pocket and used to pull them out, even when I first met him, to jot down random items. *Buy bread. Read diabetes article. Check title of Danny Kaye movie where he dresses up in armor.* He told me early on that this was how he stayed organized, living a life on the road as he did: when he got home in the evening—not that I knew where that home was—he'd take out the day's cards and look through them, tick off what he could from the list. Sometimes he'd use the three-by-five as a notecard, writing a quick letter to his mother or his sister, or now and then to Sarah, then pop it in an envelope and get it into the mail. *Dear Sarah,* I saw him write once, *What's it like to know Russian? Do you feel like a spy from a 1980s movie, the kind with lots of red lighting and thick accents? I hope you don't end up on a submarine in foreign waters. Try not to go under. Love, Richard.*

He started writing some of these to me, and he'd leave me two or three before heading off for the week. Sometimes they were very short and sweet: *Angel: Keep smiling!* Or *I'll think of you till I see you.* Sometimes they were obscure: *Angel, if you land on the Community Chest, try to pick the Get Out of Jail Free card as those always come in handy.* Sometimes playful: *Angel, I hold you closer to my heart than my first cup of coffee in the morning.* Every now and then Richard gave me a card I was fairly sure he had meant to keep for himself: *Script idea: guy dreams nightly of space travel, a moonwalk. One morning he wakes up to discover a strange other-planetary rock by the side of the bed; rock has magical powers.*

I collected these notes (*Angel, the thought of your smile keeps me going through a long day; Angel, thank you for working for Mr. Finkelstein because if you didn't I'd never have met you, and that's a terrible thought*) and put them, where else, in an envelope. I kept the envelope in my purse. It, the envelope, was one of Richard's, a yellow five-by-eight, bigger than it needed to be, but in its way a form of disguise, because it wasn't pink or perfumed, it looked like an envelope for business, not pleasure. But in my saying that, you can see the guilt beginning to creep up on me, like salt markings left by the tide, and though I might have tried to brush it off, dismiss it—What? I haven't done anything! I just have a new friend here, and God knows I needed one—the inner voice, the one that might not have believed in the universe's wisdom per se but knew perfectly well that some actions were righter than others—well, that voice was saying sternly: Watch out. Watch out here. Keep an eye on what you're doing. Don't—the inner voice was clear on this—don't do something you will have to spend the rest of your life regretting. You've done that before, and look where it got you.

Nonetheless, when Richard finally one day suggested we take a walk in the park together, I could only say yes. More accurately I gulped yes, like a fish out of water, eager for oxygen. "That sounds great!" When he clarified that he would come back at the end of my work day to meet me, saying he could not stay long just then as he had a new account in a subdivision to visit, I blanched. My heart performed a brief acrobatic act, a cartwheel or backflip. The end of the day was dangerous, and I knew it: husbands were, generally, released then and allowed back into circulation. But Richard was holding a walk in the park out in his hand like a piece of peanut brittle, my favorite candy, and it was as though I hadn't tasted sugar in months. I could not imagine having the will or strength to say no to this offer. A walk in the park. My big leprechaun near me. Maybe there would be a moment when I could fold myself into his large, warm embrace.

I said yes.

And when the round Finkelstein clock showed five-thirty I reminded myself that my husband never left work before six, and I told Richard nervously that I could not stay out long. "That's fine," he said, once again as though there were nothing untoward about what we were doing, which made me wonder if perhaps this walk in the park was not at all what I was thinking, but was actually something dry and innocent: a walk in the park, simply, a chance for Richard to run by me some business proposal, some envelope favor.

But no sooner had we cleared the stretch of commerce around the stationery store—café, bookstore, the fragrant caves of Tibet— when Richard, in his conversational way, said to me, "Angel—tell me what's in your heart."

The organ in question performed another gymnastic trick, invisibly. "What do you mean?" I stalled. Now that he was broaching the subject, the subject of hearts and their contents, I felt a sudden surge of nostalgia for all our conversations about everything else. Wait—first tell me something else about Chicago! Let's go back to the subject of your third or fourth girlfriend, the one whose mother kept calling you Robert by mistake! Remind me about the time your sister broke three plates, trying to learn how to juggle!

"Something," Richard said philosophically, gently, as he steered me in the direction of the park, "has brought us together. There is some reason we met, you and I." His face was fond, but solemn.

"Chance?" I tried faintly, but I was too polite, too encouraging, to speak the rest of the sentence that crouched in my mind. *Because Milton died and you were the appointed heir to the envelope operation. And because my husband decided long ago I'd be safer in stationery than scribbling entries in my incomplete dictionary.*

"No, no." Richard was laughing, like I had made quite a good joke. "This wasn't chance, this meeting. Look at how we talk. Look at how we have gotten to know each other so quickly, like we knew each other before, somehow."

It was true, it did feel like that. I turned a blind ear to the sound of a past-life reference.

"It's so easy to talk to you. It's so easy to be with you. You can meet a thousand people in this world you don't feel that way about."

I hardly met anyone those days, except the nameless customers and occasional adult functionaries relating to Alan and Ryan, but I was sure Richard was right. It had to be a rarity, this spark, this light between us.

"I think there was some purpose to our meeting. There's some larger scheme here. The universe doesn't make mistakes."

That old chestnut. He had shared this view before, I recalled. And however caught up I was in that moment with Richard, in his fervency, his amorous tone (I would have to call it that), I could not stem the flow of interior questions and contradictions. What about Hiroshima? Hitler? I wanted to ask him. Terrible film remakes, bad novels, reality TV? Didn't we all have to admit the universe slipped up from time to time, out of carelessness or spite? Didn't we hapless human beings collude, more often than not, in those egregious errors?

"What do you think the purpose to our meeting is?" I asked Richard, instead of the above. By now my head and heart both were jumping around. I loved Richard, yes, and was thrilled that he seemed to be on his way to making a declaration of some kind. Then, too, the idea terrified me. I wasn't as far gone, as far over the cliff of fixation as I had pretended to myself in my 3 A.M. fantasies. "I mean—I'm married." Somebody had to mention it.

"I know," Richard sighed as we entered the park. And there is the green and ease of a park, the trees and grass, the dogs and the kid-shouts, that make even a troubled heart calmer. I felt better there in the green, like this exciting, strange conversation with Richard would somehow work out all right. My husband's optimism, I guess, that mad strain: I had some of it, too. "But I find myself wondering," he murmured, "what's possible between us."

It was a soft, open-ended statement. He was not asking, not demanding; he was just wondering. And couldn't I be honest with myself? I had been wondering, too, as I collected Richard's notes and endearments, as I felt his phantom limbs around me when I lay next to my husband, as I sketched improbable meetings or encounters in which Richard's uncle-ish facade fell away and something hungrier, lover-like, emerged instead. I had wanted to touch him. Hadn't I? So—what was possible?

"I am already so besmirched," I told Richard obscurely, but if anyone could handle obscurity, Richard could. I was thinking of Theresa, and the boys, and the way my husband had seduced me (the way I had allowed him to)—secure in his confidence that the sun of righteousness would shine on us again eventually after the dim adulterous stretch was forgotten, when in fact we had never managed to wash the adulterous stain out of our marriage, no matter how many damned times I did the laundry. The boys were living, walking proof of the disaster, and though I pretended to find them tiring and boy-annoying, it was also the case that I pitied them, those boys, their DDT of a mother and their strangled joint-custody arrangements, and even their dealings with a father who loved them but was increasingly eaten up by anxiety and rage.

All those stains. All of it, stain. And we hadn't even gone further back in my life, to the part before my husband, when I lived on the other side of the bay, in that place near the mountain, where had occurred so many of my earlier errors. My abandonings. The ones that had gotten me started on my Dictionary of Betrayal.

"Oh," Richard said, affection thickening his voice. "You shouldn't talk that way." He held my hand. Held my hand! Walked us over to the bench like we were a regular couple, like we had nothing to worry about. "You aren't besmirched, Angel." That same gentle voice. What a balm. Like he was God, or the Pope, capable of absolution. "I don't see a single smirch on you." He pretended to look.

I thought of a question Richard had once asked me over lunch, about my Dictionary. He had asked me out of the blue, right after finishing telling me some story about playing baseball as a kid, and how he made a great play that had saved the game, catching a fly ball in blindingly bright sunlight, "Are you writing your Diction-ary—" he had used the present tense, I noticed, like it was still a work in progress, "from the point of view of the betrayer or the betrayed?" "Both," I had said, to keep it simple, but in this park, in this dusk, holding this man's hand now, I wanted to say to him— *Betrayer.* BETRAYER. I write from the point of view of the betrayer. It is so much easier to be the one who's betrayed. You get the clean sheets and the high ground, you get the gold star of the victim. Being a betrayer is the one you never get over. You can never erase it from the record. No amount of traffic school or community serv-ice will wipe out the violations. They are always there, written. The ink is indelible.

I wanted to tell Richard this, and more, the story about the mountain, and what happened near there—it was the next logical step in the exchange, to go back to that grief. But something hap-pened to stop me. An asteroid hit the earth, shaking the ground profoundly and causing the trees over our heads to light brightly on fire. Or perhaps it was an earthquake, a temblor, the 8.6 at last, the one they had told us for years to expect. The gas lines breaking and erupting into flame. A disaster raging all round us, in a matter of minutes.

Or maybe it was just my husband.

After a moment I realized that, actually, it was just him. Just him! He had found Richard and me sitting on the park bench, side by side, holding hands, and the jealous explosion pretty well engulfed us. "What is going ON here? Who the hell are YOU?" My husband bolted over from the sidewalk, a blur of limbs and fury. I felt myself grabbed at and yanked up like a bad child being pulled away from mischief and evil and thrown in the general direction of the vehicle which waited curbside, like a cop car, to take me handcuffed away. Richard, who in a further minute might have been scorched to ash, somehow escaped, alive and still clothed, to find safe haven elsewhere. As he left, a shower of curses rained down like arrows on his head, and the promise, "I'll come after you with a hatchet!" made its way into the air.

I did not manage a goodbye to Richard. I did not know when I'd next see him.

From now on, I guessed, we'd be back to just my husband and me. Just the two of us. No third party at all.

Oh, *hallelujah*.

Stage Set

Counterintelligence — Don't, if you're trying to figure out what's going on, go too far down the espionage route. It is inadvisable to track cell phone records, search bags or purses, or hack into a spouse's e-mail. You never know what can of worms you'll open if you do. If your spying activities are discovered, don't be surprised if false leads are then planted where you will come across them, e.g. searches that may show up in the spouse's browsing history for items such as "Divorce lawyers with reasonable fees."

⟶

So I'll tell you something. If you live with someone who's perpetually grouchy—if his tirades are the arias of your days and the swan songs of your nights—you become something like immune to his rage, even when the volume goes up exponentially and you yourself are now the prompt for the bitterness and expletives. When my husband shouted at and denounced me in the days that followed the park bench, I stiffened and held firm, as against a strong wind or an unpleasant odor. I was not as affected as you might have thought. He did not lay a hand on me (to his credit, I suppose you could say, in the jungle context of marriage and its primitiveness), but his words whipped and lashed, and his voice might have brought down the condo if the place hadn't been up to code with seismic reinforcements. But as he hollered and ranted, I sat still in my electric chair, on my hot seat, and every door within me closed, one after another, until I was just very quiet and alone right in the center, in the all-white cell at the heart of me, hardly even listening, waiting for the extreme weather to pass.

When it did pass, though, things got worse. In retrospect the storms were quite bracing. Their tragic aftermath was harder. When the worst of the hurricanes blew over—the debris scattered around us, broken plates, a smashed phone, paper torn into tiny confetti—*that's* when I got scared. You'll pardon the mixed meteorological metaphors I hope, but sometimes my husband's demeanor led the imagination more toward fire and earthquake (appropriately enough as we live in the West), and at other times we were somewhere more tropical, it seemed, the Gulf Coast perhaps, with the feeling of battering winds and floods of emotion. After which, calmer, spent, my husband became a sad piece of wreckage himself, and I had to come out of my shelter at last and embrace him, try to put him back together.

I hadn't expected this. I hadn't expected any of it, really, because I hadn't expected to hold Richard's hand in the park, in spite of the vividness of my 3 A.M. fantasies. As everyone knows, you can fervently picture something without thinking it could or even should actually happen. We hadn't gotten anywhere near the lurid scenarios I had allowed myself (Richard's bearded face moving across my body, Richard's hotly breathed erotic endearments in my ear, our mutual pleasures and discoveries in dim, flattering lighting, his heavy body pressing against mine). All we had done was hold hands. But to judge from the decibel level of my husband's voice, you'd have thought he had found us making love, having children, and raising a family together, right there in the park.

The decibels, as I say, did not move me. One day someone should tell the loud men of this world, and women too for that matter, that decibels never get you anywhere. They just deafen the other person, which does not ultimately help. My husband's falling apart did affect me, though. When he broke down and cried like a child, bewildered, left by its mother, there was nothing I could do but hold him and rock him and tell him I was sorry.

"It's OK," I said, holding my husband's lean frame in mine, stroking his clean-shaven cheek and chin. "Shhhhh. It's OK. It's OK." As if he'd badly scraped his knee, and after a Band-Aid and a dab of ointment, all would be well.

I was bewildered also. That made two of us. I was bewildered that this man who had appeared to experience me lately primarily as a bug in his eye or else a blind, handy receptacle for his semen, would care that much if I happened to hold an outsized leprechaun's hand. I'm not an idiot, I understand there is such a thing as possessiveness—I may not have finished it, but I did get some way into my Dictionary of Betrayal, and wrote entries on The Way People Feel They Belong to You, and Ties That Bind—but I'd have thought this came up mostly in relation to someone you actually enjoyed possessing. Someone you wanted, positively, to possess. Perhaps I underestimated the meaning for my husband of our late-night couplings; lately they had seemed perfunctory, almost biological to me, but I began to think he had infused them with more feeling than I'd been aware of. Maybe my husband mistook his endless monologues about DDT's perfidy for conversations between us. Maybe he thought we were bonding that whole miserable time. "What have I done to deserve this?" he wept one night.

"Haven't I looked after you? Taken care of you? Been a good husband?"

Well no, frankly. He hadn't. Not for quite some time. How could I tell him?

The good news, at least initially, was that I didn't have to tell him, because he wasn't interested in listening. My husband's task, as he saw it, was to expostulate. How *could* you! Who *are* you! What kind of *person*! Facts, he wanted—"Have you kissed this man? Have you gone to bed with this man? I mean, what has gone *on*, here?"— but those answers were easily enough given. No, and no, and the real answer to the last one was long and vexed, taking in the telling of tales and philosophizing over falafels, but my husband showed no signs of wanting to hear it. He did not want story: not narrative, not shading, not character, not motive. He was, like the TV watcher he had become, after images: a mirror of my former 3 A.M. self, I suppose, with his own bank of steamy sordidities he rabidly imagined and which I had to quell, one by one. No, we didn't. No, we never. For heaven's sake, we *only*. It was simply a matter of. Richard and I were—here it was, my flimsy balsawood plane, and here I was, trying to fly it—we were *just friends*.

This last, *just friends*, was rightly dismissed by my husband with a wave of the hand, but the other reassurances did, over time, lower the decibel level some. The condo no longer hourly seemed under threat of collapse, and the ringing in my ears from all the noise gradually ceased. But he would continue erratically to erupt with hot lavas of suspicion and contradiction: Why should I believe you? How do I know you're telling me the truth? What does Finkelstein know? Were you using the back room there for your liaisons? (He did use that word once, *liaisons*, which made me realize we were featuring in some newspaper article he was writing in his head. "Cheated-On Husband Murders Envelope Salesman," perhaps, with this line in the third or fourth graph: "The couple used the back room at the stationery store for their liaisons.") My husband probed and prodded, getting me to release pellets of information he could then chew on and chew on, like a cow or goat masticating purposefully. Lunch I admitted to him, for instance, though I edited down the number of visits to the Promised Land we had made from an improper dozen to a primmer, more upstanding few, but still when my husband first heard of it, fumes and steam came out of the top of his head as the magma once again became active.

"Lunch?" he yelled. "*Lunch?* What were you doing going to *lunch* with this guy? What did Finkelstein have to say about it?"

(Funny that my husband featured Mr. Finkelstein in the fatherly role, as I did. I had not realized until then the extent to which he saw Finkelstein as my bodyguard or protector.)

"Nothing. He liked Richard. He likes him," I corrected myself, using the present tense. Richard wasn't dead, after all, though my husband had made it clear to me that he would be if I had any further contact with him.

"*Liked* him?" my husband yelled again, keeping him tensed in the perfect. "What's to like? The man's a fat slob. I saw him. How could Finkelstein like him? How could anybody?"

"He's not a slob."

"He's fat. I saw him. Pillsbury Doughboy. You like that? You find that *attractive?*"

"He's just large," I told my husband, hating to hear him. This, if only he knew it, was the worst of all, worse than either the voluminous rages or the crumbling breakdowns: my husband leaning in to belittle and insult Richard. It made me hate the man I had married. If the rages left me cold and the breakdowns warm and sympathetic, the belittlings only made me wonder if I could find a number to call for some good legal advice. "Richard is substantial," I added reluctantly, hoping my husband might hear the hidden play on words, the secret reference to Richard's philosophizing, his cosmology. Maybe it was better that he didn't, though, that he took the most obvious meaning only.

"Substantial!" He issued a bitter laugh. "You could say that. The man was popping out of his suit. Eating lunch with the guy must have been a real pleasure, watching him stuff his face." There is nothing that quite matches the acid contempt the thin have for the less thin, is there?

This was the tone my husband settled on over the days, and the more comfortable he became with it—nervous mockery, caustic insult, for Richard and by extension for me, on account of my inexplicable liking or attraction—the deeper I settled into my own silent defenses of Richard, my unspoken longing for his calumnied self. As a technique to realign my affections, if that was what he was trying to do, the belittlings were a singular failure. They may have made him feel better, though.

On the surface, I continued loyal, dutiful, contrite. I took a week off from work, using those days to clean the condo, shop for new frying pans, organize Alan and Ryan's intimate items of sporting equipment. (Those all-important cups . . . I tried not to think about them, as I tidied them away into the boxer-shorts drawer.) It is curious how housecleaning is different, depending on the angle you see it from, like one of those textured postcards that has Jesus dead on the cross if you tilt it one way and coming back to miraculous life if you tilt it the other. There are days when the scraping of dishes and folding of clothes signifies nothing except hours of a perfectly good life of the mind squandered, never to be returned: we're all going to be dead sooner than we think, and the notion that at the end you'll have to count up the hours you spent picking sauce-encrusted spaghetti off the floor when you could have been reading a great Russian novel or some hard gems of modernist poetry is, in its way, heartbreaking. On the other hand, when troubles are roiling within you, it must be admitted that housework can soothe. It is repetitive, quiet, predictable (as Richard might have said, there is a Zen in the monotony), and in its own uncomplicated way—*good*. You can never be faulted, morally, for picking up dirty clothes or putting away glassware. Rather, you are helping, you are doing your job, you are performing a service, you are being a good wife, stepmother, woman. The words my husband had been flinging at me about Richard were, needless to say, reminding me again of the land of shame and condemnation, and so to inhabit the country of housewife drudgery instead was a kind of spiritual vacation. Furthermore, no one can deny the basic pleasure in the physical result: your surroundings restored to something like order can only make you feel closer to sanity, if not God.

The difference now being that my husband insisted on hanging around, too. He took several days off from his job (at a rather sensitive time, given the pressures on him for performance) in order to be by my side, to prove his devotion as a husband once more, and—incidentally—keep me within eyeshot so I could not go off and have any secret *liaisons* with my fat slob of a love object. My husband did not trust me, it was clear, as far as he could throw me, and so for the first time in five years I had the rare opportunity to watch the man make a stab at genuine domestic partnership. It was strange and touching, like seeing him in drag. I watched his hands scrubbing pots, his unfamiliar fingers fiddling with dials on the front of machines he had never been friendly with. One evening he even manfully tried to cook stew, and if the meat had the texture of saddle leather there was nonetheless a sweetness to it that came from good intentions. (And the children, to their credit, were minimal in their torments, somehow sensing the momentousness of the occasion and managing to down a bowl each without sarcasm or complaint. They could be good boys when they had to be.)

I can't pretend I didn't relish it, this division of kitchen labor I had for so long been harping on about, and it did restir the coolish embers of wifely feeling I had for my husband. We were making love frequently in those days, nightly, so he could mark out his territory again and again, and I will say that after eating a meal made for me by my husband's own hands I felt differently about those hands touching me, lean though they were. I had some affection for them, even. And I wanted to make the man feel better. That urge was still there, in fact had never, even with all the angry arias and swan songs, gone away. I cared about my husband and wanted to help him. Lord knows I did not actively want to hurt him. The spark had not lit between Richard and me so I could singe my husband and blacken his spirit. At least, I didn't think that had been the genesis of it. If Richard and I had met for a reason, as some people were known to believe, it was not for the purpose of torturing my husband. That had been incidental. Collateral damage, as our hyena-faced president might have said. Really, all I had wanted for myself was some measure of escape.

The only person who would understand any of this, of course, was Richard, and I was not allowed to think of him, breathe him, see his name written on the inside of my eyelids, imagine his kind face, hear his friendly voice in my inner ear . . . let alone talk to him.

We have by now circled back to where I first started the story, to the place where Richard, as religion, as revolutionary, as obscenity, was banned from our police state of a union, and my husband, as chief enforcer, was constantly monitoring and spying in an attempt to catch infractions. In the first days after the park-bench incident I had been naive enough to place a few telephone calls to Richard to say hello, to make sure he was all right; we had never spoken on the phone before but this was the modern world, he did have a cell phone and I did have its number. Subsequently, though, I received a furious printout from my husband, who was using his computer to monitor all telephonic communications. "Is this *him?*" my husband shouted at me, pointing a thin finger at an incriminating, repeating number. "This is him, isn't it? Doughboy?" I stopped making those calls.

What gulag awaited if I violated the protocol was not made clear to me, but in a certain way gruel and hard labor out on the steppes held some appeal, so forlorn did I feel without being able to see my good-hearted, red-haired guy. This was maybe the flawed, romantic thinking of someone trapped in a stationery store and an undernourished marriage, who was constitutionally incapable of counting her blessings. I should have settled for the undernourished marriage, right? Should have put up with the plaid living-room set without complaint. I should not have sought substance in the form of a nice guy who sold envelopes and told amusing stories about his past. Why couldn't I be content with what I had? Why had I allowed lunches at the Promised Land to turn my head?

As I say, the only person who could have helped me answer this damned question was Richard himself. How I missed him. How I *missed* him: you would not believe; my husband would not have believed. It was like—there must be a country and western song about this—a gaping hole in my heart. A big cannonball had gone through me, emptying me out. I was missing something crucial. I was missing my friend. I wanted to talk to him. Goddamnit! *I wanted to talk to him*. He would have understood; he would have made me feel better. He always had the ability to make me feel better.

I did go back to the stationery store after a week. Normal life had to resume. And my husband could not continue the sensitive stay-at-home-man lark for more than a few days—which was just as well as he'd managed to shrink my favorite sweater and scratch nonstick pans with metal spatulas, and had one night cooked a chicken casserole colored a radioactive yellow from saffron he had tossed in by the whimsical fistful. On balance my husband's new contributions, though in some way salving of my spirit, were wreaking havoc in an area of married life he was, it was clear, not cut out for. No. It was time for him to go back to his wicked co-workers, who would no doubt have schemed and connived in his absence, time for him to try once again, heroically, to fend off the inevitable. And if he was going back to work he was going to make sure I was too. The Envelope Affair may, perilously, have carried on at my place of employment, but by this point my husband had been dissuaded from his fixation on liaisons in the back room and had reverted to thinking of Finkelstein as a helpful chastity belt. He actually walked me to work that first morning, as he had in the sentimental old days, time of frothy cappuccinos and fragrant rosehip teas, dropping me off with Finkelstein like a parent hand-ing a toddler over to daycare. "She's been a bit under the weather," my husband lied. "So she should take it easy. I've packed her a lunch so she doesn't have to venture out in this cold." Mr. Finkel-stein nodded approvingly, of course, as a guy who bristled at the idea of squandering dollars on overpriced deli sandwiches, and if he understood the code in my husband's comments, he was dis-creet enough not to let on. (Had Finkelstein seen Richard and me go out for a walk that fateful afternoon? Had he wondered?) It was true that my husband had assembled food for me in a cute brown-paper bag. It made me think of all the lunches I had made over the years for my husband's precious Alan and Ryan (the squeeze-yogurts! the bagels!), and I paused over this landmark, a lunch made by my husband's own hands, for *me*. It was only later that I discovered my husband's lack of adeptness with mayonnaise, as I bit into a mushy tuna-fish sandwich that oozed with the stuff, and

found a note dropped in near the apple that read DON'T FORGET
WHAT YOU PROMISED. I LOVE YOU. HAVE A GOOD DAY.

There was a sadness and a sweetness in that note, in that apple.
I ate till I was full, though I was still hollow-hearted. My husband
was willing to tell me, sincerely, that he loved me and wanted to
repair our marriage; but he did not once think to ask me why the
envelope guy had meant something to me, what pocket of loneli-
ness there was within me that that fat fellow (my husband could
not let go of the size issue) might have filled.

And then, a few days later, he searched my bag, and found the
notes written to *Angel*.

It had not occurred to me to hide them. You can see, I hope, in
my stupidity, a certain innocence: there was a way in which I continued to feel that it had not been wrong, this friendly man coming
with me to the Promised Land to offer me solace over falafel and
pita bread. All right, we held hands and perhaps shouldn't have;
and one day, that last day, Richard had a light in his eye that
strictly speaking did not belong in the look of a man toward a
woman who was married. The park-bench incident was, I'll admit,
questionable. But before that, all had been kindness and affection,
nothing more, and Lord knows I had felt starved for both.

"But these are LOVE LETTERS!" my husband roared, holding
them, crumpled, before my pained, tearing eyes. "The man was in
love with you! It says so *right here*! How could you *allow* this?" He
did not wait for an actual answer, but simply concluded: "That
does it. We're going to Puffin."

I had thought it might come to Puffin, eventually. Disaster on
this scale usually did. My husband might sound in most respects

like a regular guy, with the TV watching, the suit, the bad temper; but where we live, in the West, even a regular guy has to have some kind of emotional vocabulary and be willing to go to a counselor when crisis strikes. Like the time, three years earlier, when my husband had misguidedly encouraged Theresa to visit our condo, in a spirit of rapprochement she did not happen to share, and she had furiously torn family pictures off the boys' bedroom wall and flung them onto the floor; or the time my husband agreed to co-finance, with Theresa, the purchase of her precious minivan, which led to our having to cancel, at some cost, a trip we had long planned to Hawaii. These and a few other memorable events had each sent us to Puffin.

Dr. Edward Puffin was a silver-haired, pointy-goateed man with a mild, sleight-of-hand voice, who in another setting might pass for a magician or wizard. There did seem to be a supernatural element in his work: sometimes you felt that he succeeded by hypnotizing the warring parties assembled in his room, and briefly brainwashing them into a cessation of hostilities so they could stay together for a little longer at least. He might have counted to ten then, unbeknownst to us patients, snapped his fingers, collected his hefty fee, and sent the couple on their way. Gently rearranging the furniture after one pair left so that the next two could come in to his stage set of an office, where they enacted their sad or furious kitchen-sink dramas.

When you entered this theater of negotiation, Puffin always organized his face to appear both happy and sorry to see you. He maintained a mournful cast, made more poignant by the goatee, that suggested the sense: *I regret that it has come to this*. Yet he wanted to exude reassurance. "Please, sit," he would say, with a wistful smile. "Tell me what's happening." And the language, with its seventies perfume, and Puffin himself, with his otherworldly charm, might make you think for a fanciful moment that this greeting was really the opening for a group orgy or a key-swapping party. Maybe we were going to break out of those boring fifties' conventions of fidelity and propriety, after all, explore the more modern possibilities of marriage.

"There's a guy, a fat guy, who sells envelopes."

Or maybe not.

That was how my husband began our session on a late November morning, as the gray sky glowered outside and turkeys around the country lined up for their ritual slaughter. My husband wasn't about to waste time in this emergency session. No context-setting. No gentle introductory paragraph. "She and he have been carrying on together. For *months*."

"We've been talking," I corrected. *Carrying on.* What a way to put it! How old was my husband? Ninety? He was going to have Puffin imagining *liaisons* if I didn't step in right away. "I've had lunch with him a few times."

"At work! Where she works! The guy comes in, and—*I* don't know what's gone on exactly, because she's not telling me the truth, but I know I found them sitting in a park together holding hands."

"Once," I muttered. "That happened once. That was just—"

"Holding *hands!*"

"One time! One single time."

"Now, now—" Puffin attempted, spreading out his own hands, as if the gesture would be enough to smother any irritations, all memory of the park bench.

"He's in love with her!" my husband insisted. "And—I don't know—maybe she's in love with him too. I can't get a straight answer out of her about that." He sat back on the old corduroy couch, his arms folded.

"We're friends," I insisted weakly, tossing my battered balsa-wood airplane of an excuse over to Puffin to see what he'd make of it, though even as I did so I wondered to myself, Did my husband ever ask me that question? Whether I'm in love with Richard? Did he ever come out and ask me that, actually? "I am very fond of Richard, in a friendly way." No one had to know what had happened in my head at 3 A.M. between Richard and me. That was no one's business but my own. Not even Richard had to know about that. He never had to know the comfort his large body had unreally given me, in the seamier corners of my nighttime imagination.

"Friends!" my husband expostulated. He sounded like a steam engine. The phrase *blowing a gasket* came to mind. "Then how do you explain *these*?" And from his pocket, as if he, too, were a magician, my husband pulled out some of the notes from Richard he had crumpled up earlier. It was all I could do not to grab them from him, hold them close to me, my small paper keepsakes of Richard. But my husband had a different idea of what could be done with them. "Listen to this!" he said to Puffin, as if the stage set, formerly a dull living room with a corduroy couch and a gray leather wing chair, had suddenly turned into a bar, and my husband was holding forth over a whisky. "Listen to this! 'Angel, keep smiling.' 'Angel, you're a light in my life.' 'I'll think of you till I see you.'" It was awful to hear dear Richard's blandisms in the dire voice of my husband. My face turned hot and beet colored. My palms itched. My feet sweated. "'Angel, I hold you closer to my heart than my first cup of coffee in the morning.' You tell me: are these the expressions of a *friend?*"

Puffin shook his head sorrowfully. He seemed poised, for a minute, between the barroom answer—"I say, take a shotgun and hunt the guy down, don't quit till you find him," and something better suited to corduroy and leather. He went for the latter, jutting his prim goatee in my direction, with an expression of some skepticism. "Would you like to explain your intentions with Richard?"

"None. *None.*" How could I have any intentions? My husband had put a printout of the cell phone bill on our bed for my edification. He was watching me like a hawk. The word "hatchet" had been mentioned. If I had a hole in my heart the size of a cannonball from missing Richard, what of it? What could I do about it? "Whatever connection there was for a while," I said, "it's over."

"Can you honestly say you've put your feelings for Richard behind you?" Puffin pressed. His goatee looked prickly. I was beginning to hate him. I was beginning to hate them both. I wanted a change of scenery. This drama—*this* one—I was tired of.

"I've had to," I lied. But why not lie, at this point, for all the good truth would have done me? "It was only—" It is hard to resist, though, finally, in these sessions. The urge to tell your side of the story. "It was only an escape, for a little while. From his worries about his job." I gestured toward the man sitting next to me on the couch. "From his complaints about Theresa. From our concerns about the boys."

Puffin turned back to my husband, to watch the ball land in his court. Really, sometimes these sessions were just that: tennis matches. There were periods when all Puffin had to do was watch. And that short feeder I'd given was enough to set my husband off on one of his familiar deliveries, the oiliness of his co-workers, the heavy threats of the incompetent management, and the wicked, unending ways Theresa was bleeding us dry. "She sent me a bill for the fucking *plumber!*" my husband shouted. He was like a dog who has stopped barking at a pigeon only to find a squirrel to harass instead. "Said she couldn't pay it. Wants *me* to, for Christ's sake."

Puffin continued his sorrowful nodding.

And on went the litany, and out went my gaze, through the window, to some unnamed potted plants standing around Puffin's small cement patio. There they were, half shaded but climbing up toward the sunlight. Phototropism, they call that, I recalled from high school biology. Turning toward the light. That was what it had been with Richard, I wanted to explain to these two stupid men, my husband, Puffin, whichever would listen. Really, it was just that after all those years in the damned dark—*You've ruined my life! Who the hell are these people to threaten my job? Boys—come on now, boys, show some respect to your stepmother!*—I was after some light. The spirit lift of conversation, with a man who was interested in questions of morality and his old friend the universe.

Let me explain something here, as someone who has worked on a Dictionary of Betrayal and spent some quiet moments behind the counter reflecting on virtue and its opposites, while customers were busy browsing for staple replacements or chuckling over bad jokes in the card section. Given the righteous bombs Theresa had lobbed our way over the years—*You ruined my life!*, as noted—I had to find places to shelter so that my sense of self as a decent person basically (certainly not Pol Pot, or Hitler), was not turned to ash. Theresa's unending tragedy as the abandoned first wife had gradually depleted my husband and me of our natural resources: money and humor, time and heart, empathy and patience.

And though I complained about all the sports practices and fart jokes, the fact was that one place I did take shelter, paradoxically, was in looking after those two boys when they were with us. Alan and Ryan. To hear my husband's account of it, before he met me his and DDT's children were being raised in a household empty of honesty or companionship; with me, he was hoping, so he claimed, to give the boys some haven of conjugal love and respect.

Had we managed it, that haven? Was divorce one of the world's necessary evils, like a forest fire, doing important rebalancing work even as it ravages, and those of us who encounter it must just be positive and brave—in which case it was Theresa, not us, who had the black mark against her as it was she who had, with such determination, dragged all of us downer and downer?

I thought of Millie, suddenly. Our old neighbor friend. She was one of the people closest to me as I grew up. She taught me how to play gin rummy; when she was cooking hot dogs, she'd cook an extra one for me; she had a heart full of kindness and grace. My mother had herself recently divorced at the time, and Millie was on hand to prove that such cataclysms were survivable, that good humor was recoverable, that small eruptions of confusion after were forgivable. There was nothing you could do, nothing mischievous or wayward, that Millie couldn't understand. Living next to us there in the shadow of the blue mountain, across the bay from where I now lived with my husband, Millie had seemed to me a person made entirely of light. After she was gone I never felt comforted, brightened, in the same way again.

Until Richard. Richard had some of that same quality in him. He had a full, bearded face of acceptance, as if there was nothing you could say that would shock or upset him. As if he had room, time, for all of it. For any of it. For your words, your sadness, the griefs you nurtured, misguidedly. Without Richard I'd be flung back to where I was supposed to be, into the arms of my husband, who tolerated only what he felt he had to, who did not listen to anything he didn't like the sound of, who had half a mind to condemn me, now, along with the others on his long list. Somewhere in my husband's speechifying (not that I was paying much attention), he had seen fit to link Theresa's ill-treatment of him with my own—as if my "carrying on" with Richard was some kind of equivalent to the years of vitriol and hatred aimed at him by his ex-wife. As if it had never occurred to my husband: the irony of himself, a known adulterer—that guy who struck up a conversation with the girl in the café—expressing such intense moral outrage at the imagined adultery perpetrated by someone else. By *me*.

"He used to say he wanted to keep me like a key," I said softly in the direction of the plants. "He wanted to put me in his pocket."

"What?" Puffin turned to me.

I had not even intended to speak. The words came out of me, unwilled. "He said he was going to keep me safe, warm, and happy."

Puffin tilted his head like a dog, then shook it slowly, back and forth. "Well, that's an unreal promise, isn't it?" he opined gently. "The fellow was trying to tempt you—to hold out something impossible."

Puffin thought I was talking about Richard, I realized. He did not know the lines had come from my husband, back around the time we had met. The therapist gestured toward the man sitting next to me. "Your husband, here, won't diminish you—he won't pretend to you like that. Your husband is what's real."

The tears that came to my eyes then did not seem to worry Puffin. They gratified him, rather. "You see?" he said modestly, as part of his wrap-up. We were running out of time. He was still facing me, but watching my husband. "I think she's sad for the hurt she has caused you." Then he returned to me. "Isn't that right?"

Rather than explain the complexity of the saltwater on my face—my memory of my husband's fond, early words and Puffin's condemnation of them here; and then, beyond that, Millie, Richard, and the light—I chose to nod, humbly. It was easier that way. I could give Puffin the illusion that he had earned his fee.

"She understands the friendship was foolish. She regrets the harm done," Puffin continued, ventriloquizing me inaccurately. He was moving toward a good ending here. He was working toward *closure*. It was one of the important arts of his profession. "And I think I'm right in saying—aren't I?—that she will have no more truck with Richard."

I looked down somberly, a motion that could have been construed as a nod by someone who was looking for agreement. I did not say anything. I was not going to commit myself further. But that head dip was enough for my husband to pull out his checkbook with a mollified expression, as he prepared to drain our bank account yet further to fund this expensive but, as he saw it, vital investment in our marital future, and Puffin sat back serenely, satisfied by another job well done.

A Hard Place

Special dispensations — Being diseased, pregnant, or un-employed are no guarantees that your spouse will not cheat on you. It's surprising, but there it is.

⎯⤙⎯

The ax fell the week after.

It was ugly and terrifying, and not altogether unlike the sky careening down on our heads, or our fragile shelf of the state falling into the Pacific, as certain climatologists will have you believe is one day inevitable. On the other hand, there was also an element of relief when it finally happened. In its biting, antsy distraction the anticipation was worse than the cold hard hit of the event itself.

In our happy-ever-after condo my husband and I were a mile or two up from the train tracks, though you were rarely aware of the trains in the day, with the noise, chaos, and heartbreak of the surrounding commerce. But at night, when a deeper quiet reigned, the late-hour howl of the train had that haunting, provocative melancholy, and when I used to lie awake next to my husband there were two sorts of imaginings I had. In one, the train was coming to take me away from my vexed domestic entanglement (OK, possibly with Richard: possibly he and I together could find some peace, some respite, in an unspecified elsewhere). In another scenario, the train was an unemployment train, a getting-fired train, and it was about ready to jump the tracks and come find my husband, whose time had now come.

He told me in a phone message. I didn't use my telephone while working—if there was one thing that exercised Finkelstein and me both it was those twenty-year-old clerks on their phones who act as though taking your money for purchases was the most irritating interruption imaginable—but I did have it with me in case of emergency. I've found the cell phone generally an over-rated instrument, as its main function seems to be to ruin people's manners and limit yet further a person's opportunities for solitude and reflection; but that kind of view places me squarely in the twentieth century, perhaps even the nineteenth, an era I have read about and wistfully considered my properer spiritual home. Yet here I am stuck in the twenty-first, with its countless smart, shrinking gadgets and melting polar ice caps. Better make the best of it.

My husband called me and left a message. I saw the readout on the screen informing me that someone had called—the thing about these wretched implements is they feel they have to tell you *everything*, just as soon as it's happened—and enjoyed a brief flutter of hope that it might be Richard, whose voice I had been desperate to hear. But sure enough it was my husband, who was, let's be honest, just about the only person who ever called me. I figured it might be Don't forget Ryan has piano this afternoon, or Could you get some more Tums, so I didn't listen right away. Eventually I snatched a moment when Mr. Finkelstein was busy trying to coax some bewildered novelist type into remembering which number ink-jet cartridge was the right one for her printer, and I disappeared into the back room. The famous back room, home of terrible-tasting coffee and putative liaisons.

"The company announced its job cuts today. Nice timing, eh? Right before Christmas." My husband sounded like he was giving a short, bitter public speech. Then, in a voice of some exhaustion, more personally: "I'm on the list to go. The severance package is decent but not princely. We'll be able to get by for a while. I've got twenty-four hours to clear out my desk. I think," he concluded, heavily, "I'm going to go out with some of the other losers for a drink. Don't expect me back for dinner."

A pit opened up in the bottom of my stomach. Even if I had expected it. Even if I felt thankful, perversely, that the waiting was over. But if my husband had been rageful before, awaiting this betrayal and disaster—what would he be like now that it had come to pass, his worst fears confirmed? And what did "get by" mean in real terms? Would we start sweating blood even worse, over money?

When I spoke with him after work, as I walked back to our condo—past the café, and the bookshop, and the fragrant caves of Tibet—my husband sounded surprisingly unruffled. He sketched a few details. He was methodical in his explanation of the amount of pay he would still get, and for how long. His voice was uncannily low and quiet and he sounded as though he was speaking on a pre-recorded loop, repeating stale information. He apologized for not being there that evening for Alan and Ryan, but I was the good wife and stepmother and said it was fine, I could handle it, he should go out with his friends. People who had just weeks ago been potential backstabbers in my husband's dim firmament had suddenly become fellow victims and buddies, guys he'd be happy to down a few beers with. Misery loves company.

So on that December evening the three of us paddled in our small lifeboat together. After the carpooler dropped the boys off, I told them their dad had had bad news at work, and they were old enough to have a wracking sense of the remark's import. Their dark little faces—the faces of people who were neither children nor adults but trapped in the uncomfortable twilight zone in between—contracted around contours of glum worry I recognized from their father. (Genes will out, however fiercely the Theresas of this world wish the damn things could be disavowed.) It would be fine eventually, I bluffed to the boys, who knew full well I was bluffing, but there might be some changes ahead. Alan immediately wondered whether his mother would have to sell back the minivan, and Ryan, thinking of some movie or sitcom, asked if his dad would start lying around all day at home in his bathrobe. I issued blanket denials to these and other nervous questions. I produced bowls of the great American comfort food, macaroni and cheese, and then I urged us into routine, that global consoler, telling Ryan to practice for his piano lesson and Alan to get out his homework. And a couple of successful hours passed in this way, Ryan plonking out "Go Tell Aunt Rhody" on the upright while I coached Alan on an inane assignment for his French class in which he had to describe a famous person's likes and dislikes. *Monsieur le Président*, Alan came up with, on his own, showing rare filial unity with his father in translating sentiments he'd heard growled by the fist-shaking latter in front of the TV, *n'aime pas lire, ni les journaux ni les livres, et il n'aime pas écouter ce que les autres lui dit.* I helped him some, I admit, with the ordering of the words. *Il aime regarder le football et les filmes des "cowboys."* The smirk of enjoyment Alan showed writing all this was normally not something I'd sanction, but these were special circumstances. He wanted to add, *"Le Président est un idiot!"* but I told him it was not part of the assignment to make judgments of that kind.

By the time the boys were toothbrushed and pajamaed and playing an especially vicious game of Monopoly in their bedroom—Alan the brute boot, Ryan the hyper racecar, me the hapless cruise ship, tooting slowly around the board—we had all but forgotten about the other guy, who came home close to bedtime. There was a collective tensing as we heard the front door open, the clank of keys thrown down on the counter, shoes slipped off and cluttered onto the floor (where I would trip on them in the morning, as usual; it was one of the habits I was trying and failing to break in my husband). There was a squeak of the refrigerator door opening, a pause, then its closing again, followed by the scary-movie sound of slow, heavy footsteps coming down the hall. A few heavy pulsing cellos just then would have formed a suitable soundtrack to our racing hearts.

My husband put his face in the doorway. Not his body. Just his face. It had an inebriated sag, his cheeks having abruptly gone bloodhoundish, as if all this time he had kept his muscles tight and sober to give the impression he was doing a good job. Was indispensable. Was at the top of his game. There was no need for any of that pretense anymore; gravity and disappointment could be yielded to, at last. It was an affecting transformation.

"Hi, guys," he said from the doorway. He was leaning, I now saw, rather weightily on the frame itself.

"Hi, Dad." The boys spoke together, their voices small but aiming for normalcy.

"Who's winning?"

"I am," Alan said, and Ryan nodded his agreement (which was ironic, as mere minutes earlier they'd been close to fisticuffs as they compared quantities of money).

"He's got Park Place and Broadway," I clarified. "Me, I've only got Vermont and Connecticut Avenues, and I'm mortgaged up to the hilt."

"Try to stay ahead of the game, there, Alan," my husband said. "You're a winner." This strange, bland peppiness didn't sound the least bit like my husband. It seemed like a line from a script of a movie about a different man altogether, in quite different circumstances. "I'm going to bed now, boys. It's been a long day."

"Good night, Dad."

"Good night." But his voice had already retreated some distance, like a voice on the radio you are turning down so you can hear the person in the room with you who is trying to ask you a question.

It went on like that for days. Alan and Ryan went back to their mother's, of course, and life in the minivan, while at our condo an eerie calm reigned. There was no shouting. There was little bitterness. There was the watching of television, predictably, mind-numbing collections of talking heads debating congressional inadequacies, or a golf tournament somewhere that caught my husband's attention, men in tidy shirts grimacing as they gazed toward the obscure rough, or raising a proud fist when they popped the white ball into its cup. (I am in an American minority, I suppose, in believing that the life metaphors yielded by sports-watching are more demoralizing than not.) I tried to do my bit during the watching by rubbing my husband's shoulders and agreeing easily to sex after. It was the least I could do to comfort him, soothe his bruised ego.

There was also, as you might expect, the use of the Internet for surprising new purposes. My husband spent some time browsing online shopping opportunities, kitchen gizmos we'd never use, gadgets to take the pits out of cherries or machines to deep fry whole turkeys. Once when I was at work he placed an order for four personalized Christmas stockings made of velvet and genuine alpaca, at what cost I didn't like to ask. For several days he went on a *Where are they now?* kick, looking up people he'd gone to high school with, which produced the customary mixed bag, fate having delivered its haphazard fortunes. "Look at this!" my husband said one night from behind a white screen. "Bryan Kessler writes for *TV* now! He works on that office comedy that's such a big hit. He always was a smart alec." Another day it was, with some satisfaction, "I see Tom Fenton's start-up tanked." He squinted at the story. "That guy was an arrogant bastard. Football star. They're the worst." Inevitably, one tragic afternoon, a low, ghoulish whistle came from behind the screen. "Hey, what do you know?" As if I were really listening; as if he were really even talking to me. "April Lee is dead. Meningitis, for Christ's sake. How do people get that?

Is it contagious?" He tsked, under his breath, then added, distantly, "She was so pretty. I remember her."

In this period going to the stationery store was, more than ever, a godsend. I felt pity for my husband and at the same time wanted to flee from him. There was an irony here, in that it was, of course, my husband who had set me up with Mr. Finkelstein in the first place. The station that was meant initially to take me away from the dark, circular wanderings of my Dictionary of Betrayal, and be a bright distraction during the long hours of my husband's worka-day absence, had gradually transformed into a haven away from that same husband's demanding presence. I felt safe there, with all the card stock and nylon file folders and sheets of sticky-backed gold stars. It was an ordered environment. Peaceful, even. You wanted to make sure that shifty teen wasn't going to pocket some pens without paying for them, and you had to listen to two tow-headed kids fighting over the last box of scented markers, and every now and then there might be a dispute involving the time of the express-mail collection. But generally we had peace in the sta-tionery store, not least because of Mr. Finkelstein himself, a model of taciturnity, that quality undervalued in our ever-louder world. You could count on Finkelstein to keep quiet. He was not going to bug you. He had his pet peeves—including overpriced gourmet coffee and people who forgot to close the door behind them on a cold day—but in the main he kept his opinions to himself.

The problem was, my husband started showing up there. At the stationery store. Sometimes just to pop in and say hi, as if he were in the middle of several important errands, though his purpose-lessness hung around him like an odor. He professed to be worried that I might be lonely, and one day he got it into his head to suggest we go out to lunch. He said it as though it were a very sweet, romantic idea, but underneath his sincerity-shellacked exterior I was fairly sure I saw an eerie glimmer either of aggression—*You let that fat slob take you to lunch, didn't you?*—or desperation—*I'm your husband, aren't I, and even if I'm unemployed can't you let me take you to lunch?*

"Where do you want to go?" I asked him evenly, putting on an accommodating expression. I was trying especially hard, in those days, to be agreeable. "The pasta restaurant has a good deal at lunchtime. You might like their linguini."

"Isn't there a place around here that sells falafel? Middle Eastern joint?" My husband tilted his head, like a bad dog trying to look cute. "That sounds just about perfect to me. How about you?" This from a man who liked his meat nice and red, who had never shown any affection for the ways of the garbanzo. It was impossible to tell whether he was toying with me or not, but the safest response was not to notice, either way.

"Sure!" I chirped. "Sounds great." As if there was nothing I'd like better than to have my husband sitting across a table from me at the Promised Land, at a seat not long since vacated by my beloved, much-missed Richard, who would have fed me Zen wisdoms and entertaining tales from his youth.

But it was a bad move on my husband's part, this, because once we were in the restaurant, what were we going to talk about? And what would I, inevitably, think about?

"I saw a meter maid," he began, getting comfortable, once we got there, "outside the stationery store a few minutes ago. She was writing up a ticket for some poor unsuspecting guy."

"Really?"

"Yeah." He shook his head. One more of the world's disappointments. "I said to her, 'So how's your job satisfaction? High? You like the feeling you get going around mugging perfectly good citizens with your nasty green envelopes?'"

"Let's take a look at the menu," I said, the way you put a crayon in the hand of a child to divert his attention. Today was not a day I felt I could dedicate to the perfidy of meter maids. But the menu didn't help much. It was as I had suspected it might be with the Promised Land's offerings: my husband was bewildered by the food described in its desert-styled script, and even after we found him some form of chicken on a skewer, he looked around with suspicion at the familiar-to-me pictures of the Dead Sea, the Wailing Wall. I could tell something sinister was snaking through his brain. I suppose I must have told him that this was my lunch spot with Richard, and so here we were, recapitulating history by lunching here together. Once again I reached for some colorful distraction.

"What news of DDT?" You can imagine how desperate I was, to ask him that.

"Oh." My husband's lips curled down, his eyes turned hard and cool as dried beans. "She knows I got the ax. I told her in an e-mail, hoping it might keep her off my back for five minutes. But of course now she's just worried about *her*. What's going to happen to the alimony, and the child support, all that shit—excuse me. I'm going to have to call the lawyers again. I bought a book, to try to understand the ins and outs of all this myself, but it's written for people who can work through all that legal language. I need a fucking interpreter."

I thought of Sarah, Richard's stepdaughter. She was going to be a translator one day. *What a peach.*

"It'll be easier just to call the lawyer," he continued. "Get into more debt there. Why not? Why stop now?"

There was a pause while I tried to think of anything else I could feed my husband, something good, something mellowing. The impulse was self-protective, partly, but also I wanted, somehow, to lift the black sag from his face. The bloodhoundish look did not suit him. I wanted to see him again with the elasticity of optimism. But finally, as a topic occurred to me—I was thinking of suggesting he take up golf, now that he had some spare time—my husband bit into his real subject, sank his teeth right in. And then he wouldn't let go.

"So what did you and the envelope guy talk about, here, over these fascinating lunches you had? What a boob your husband was? What a fool? How to get round him?"

"No." I closed my eyes. There was one day, at the table, when I had confessed to Richard: *I didn't think, when I married him, that I would be marrying Theresa too. If I had really understood that, I might have given the whole plan more thought.* But as soon as that second sentence was out of my mouth, I regretted it. I hadn't actually meant to go that far in what I said to Richard; I had not meant to lead myself, or him, into temptation. It was just that my friend's face was so sympathetic, so warm and so open. "He liked to tell me stories," I offered to my husband, looking down at my half-eaten plate of hummus.

"What kind of stories? Of all his conquests? His ventures?"

"No. Not that. Just—just—" How could I explain it to him? Some part of whatever had gone on between Richard and me had genuinely been all right. Had been sweet, and not harmful. I missed that sweetness right then; there was so much sourness and bile around. "I don't know. Stories about growing up in Chicago. Stories about—he had an interesting theory, kind of a Zen thing, about the universe." I should have known, the minute I said it, how misguided it would be to try to convey any of this to my husband.

"Did he really?" Dripping with sarcasm, and once again I had the impression, as with those wretched notes read aloud on Puffin's stage set, that poor Richard had just been stripped naked before us, exposed to mockery and slander. There was no point in my getting into the Zen element with my husband. God knows. Just leave it. Forget it. Deny everything, accede to anything, settle yourself in to your cloistered marital fate. You signed up for this, don't forget. Remember those promises you made in front of a gathering of family and friends? Remember the champagne and the flowers? *The universe doesn't make mistakes.* You promised. This, before you, is the man that you married, for better or for worse, and you'd better damn well accept it.

"I looked him up on the Internet," my husband growled, or maybe snarled. A sound that went with the bloodhound expression. "*Richard Applebee.* He once owned a party-preparation store, but it went out of business. He had to file for Chapter Eleven."

"Mmmhmmm," I said, as if I had known that, though I hadn't. My husband had enunciated "Chapter Eleven" with some satisfaction. He was building to something, but I didn't know what. Then his phone rang. "Sympathy for the Devil." "That's Michael," my husband said, frowning. One of the former backstabbers, now an unemployed soulmate. "I wonder what he wants." He snapped the thing open to find out.

"Hi, Mike. What's up? . . . You're kidding. Jesus *Christ*. I don't believe it . . . Fuck." He looked at me, rolling his eyes, shaking his head. "Sure. I'll see you there at five. No, I know. Jesus. *Fuck*." And he snapped Michael shut again. The ineffable communications of men. "Crazy company news," my husband said with a wave of his hand, like it was too complicated to go into, I'd never understand it. But whatever Michael had told him had given him new energy, and for that I was grateful. "I'm going to meet him for a drink later to talk about it. Come on. Let's get you back to work."

And he led me, after paying, the short crossed road and half block back to the stationery store. For a minute there, in command, hand under my elbow, the pilot steering his vessel, he was my old husband again, the guy I had married, and he even managed a small joke as he approached the store. "After all, you're the big breadwinner in the family now. Can't have you late back from lunch. You're the one bringing home the bacon." I liked his kidding about that, all those comforting food metaphors. I held his arm with conviction, something more definite than the hold of someone who is simply taking her fate as it comes.

When I got back to the store, Finkelstein was receiving boxes from a man in a brown uniform. "New shipment of envelopes," my boss said neutrally. "The nine-by-twelves we were low in, I placed an extra-large order. Do you want to take these to the back and unpack them?"

I swallowed and nodded, while my escort, still with me, played the helpful spouse. "Here, honey." He took a box from me. "Let me help you with those." Must you?

I wondered. Hadn't we had enough togetherness by now? But this was my husband's flypaper phase, he needed to stick with me, and I had to let him, it seemed. So off we went to the cluttered Finkelstein headquarters for our own not-so-steamy liaison. Perhaps once he saw what it was really like back there, my husband might revise his salacious fantasies; it was hard to imagine a couple maneuvering any kind of delicate position without getting themselves brained by a falling stapler or putting a knee through the coffee pot. "Let's open these," my husband said with excess cheerfulness, putting the boxes on a busy table. "Now where around here does Finkelstein keep a blade, something sharp?"

There was no mistaking the glitter in his eye.

We opened four boxes, one by one, working side by side just like the regular husband-and-wife stationery team we were not. I kept my face still throughout, as though this were any old shipment of Post-its or paperclips, but within, of course, my heart was thudding and pounding. "Just envelopes," I said breezily at the fourth one, my voice trembling slightly, though I was trying to convey an unworried, carefree attitude. What had either of us suspected, I suddenly wondered—Richard himself popping out of the cardboard like a buxom lady out of a cake?

"Oh, *look.*" It was my husband's voice, a-drip now once again with sarcasm. "What have we here?"

The interior thudding recommenced. My poor little heart. My husband was holding a small, single white envelope that did not match any of the others. I could see immediately that it was too small to contain something legitimate, like an invoice. I thought of making a grab for it, but understood that would be absurd. I was trapped. I shrugged, and folded my arms. "I don't know," I mumbled, and if you wanted to you could attach the adverb *sullenly* to the above mumble. "What is it?"

My husband made something of a show of pulling the card from its sleeve, reading it to himself first, nodding, his lips compressed into a smile that expressed, nevertheless, the inverse of a smile. He turned it toward me.

Angel, I miss you.

I took the card from his hands and tore it up, with a complicated taste in my mouth as I did it. Shame, at being caught unwittingly; fury at my husband for his theatrics; a thin wire of happiness at the sentiment expressed by the four words (I was still his Angel; I was somebody's *Angel*); and a longing to be able to say the same back in reply. *I miss you, too, Richard.* And, seeing the crumple of grief and anger on my husband's face, remorse at being the one to crumple him, and a low fear of the anger itself. The Chinese have a snack food my friends the Chen girls used to share with me when I was a kid and went along to Bruce Lee drive-ins with their family. It was an odd, savory, dried plum they called moy. The snack's taste on your tongue was simultaneously sweet, the dried plum, and the soured salt of preserve. At that moment in the Finkelstein back room my mouth tasted of something like moy.

I reached over to touch my husband, but he pulled away and tried to close himself off from me. As he turned I saw his face, and it had a crack right across it, a fissure of pain. An earthquake had hit the poor guy, had pulled him apart right at the fault line. All because of Richard: large, harmless-as-I-thought-of-him Richard.

"Everything all right?" Finkelstein put his head into the headquarters. Perhaps the silence had seemed ominous.

"Fine, just fine," I said, hoping to stave off embarrassment, and my husband simultaneously announced his departure.

"I'm just going. Got to let her get back to work. She's a busy lady, got lots going on." The crack was hearable in his voice, as if it went right through him, and I could tell Finkelstein had heard it too. I did not want my boss to have heard it and I did not want to have been the cause of it in the first place. This was a man whose pride I was trying to salvage. This was a man I cared for and lived with.

"Wait—" I said awkwardly to my husband, wanting to fix, wanting to help, but he left, not willing to risk further sentences in anyone's hearing.

So I was left to win bread for the rest of the afternoon, while suffering the slow, draining sensation that I had been punctured somewhere essential, and fluids were leaking out of me, leaving me desiccated and empty. I sold sympathy cards and address books, I helped a balding dad work the creaky copier in the corner and talked to a cloud of hairspray behind which shimmered a lady interested in printed wedding invitations. We got down the folder and looked through it, browsing fonts of various degrees of curlicued cursiveness. (*Have you really thought this through?* I wanted to ask her. *Any skeletons in anyone's closet you need to be aware of?*) When Mr. Finkelstein took his customary mid-afternoon half hour, I bought my own item from our store, a hundred three-by-five index cards, and paid for them using my employee discount. I was espe-cially sweet to customers that day—we were a good double act, Finkelstein and I, able to engage when we needed to, in spite of our unsociable exteriors—and, in the quiet lulls, I filled card after card.

Richard, I miss you too. Richard: what am I supposed to do here? My hus-band is miserable and I don't want to hurt him. Richard, I was thinking about that great story you told about raking leaves from one neighbor's lawn to another. Your early entrepreneurial days. That made me laugh. Dear Richard: are you still thinking outside the box? I find that I can't. I am trapped in this box, and I just can't think my way out of it. Richard, remind me how it is that you believe the universe doesn't make mistakes? And what happens when we do? Can we correct them? Richard, I miss you. I wish you could help me. I wish you could show me some light.

I slunk home that day. Slunk really is the only word for it. My head was bowed, my feet slid over the sidewalk, my shoulders expressed with sagging eloquence my self-loathing. I couldn't think of anywhere to turn, I couldn't think of anyone to call. (I had no interest in receiving another furious printout on the bed, no matter how strong the urge was in me to pick up the phone and dial the guy who had written me that note.) It wasn't so much a question of being between a rock and a hard place: I was *under* the rock, *inside* the hard place, both, at the same time. There was no "between" about it.

At home, I could have cleaned or I could have had a glass of wine. I chose the latter. My husband was somewhere in the wider world, drinking with Michael, the fellow ex-employee ("Fuck! Jesus!" etc.), and I didn't see why I shouldn't just sit down for once,

in my narrower world, and sip some wine. I would not cook dinner
tonight. There were no boys to perform for. Every now and then
you just want bagel chips and olives, you don't want to go anywhere near a frying pan or pasta pot. Slice off a couple of pieces of
Muenster and you're good for the night.

I sipped in the silence and tried to imagine what could be ahead
for this condo and the people within it: the grinning juvenile baseball players, faces framed by helmets, and that couple from the
photographs who were having rice thrown in their faces, never
suspecting that much worse than rice was to follow. I looked at the
handsome lean guy in the dark suit and wondered what would
happen to him if he lost his job. Would the firing present itself as
an opportunity for new growth, and turn out to be the Best Thing
That Could Have Happened? (Bookstore shelves were groaning, it
seemed, with whole volumes devoted to such stories.) Or would it,
rather—the fear that had blinked in Ryan's young eyes—lead inex-
orably to bathrobes, stubble, an increase in body odor and the tell-
tale, frequent quotation of ad taglines picked up from TV? ("Hi,
honey. Another beautiful day, it must be a Windowclean™ day!") I
thought of Millie, our old neighbor, and the gray look she wore for
a while when her husband—who was a nasty piece of work—lost
his job. It hadn't been pretty.

The phone rang. Not the real, condo telephone but the little
silver device, the one I didn't believe in, that I only carried in case
of emergencies. I looked at its over-informative panel, eager as
always to spoil surprise or suspense, and it had those seven letters,
alight, like a transcription of my own ringing, confused heart.

Richard.

I looked around, nervously—as if the refrigerator or the stove top were likely taking notes, or catching the whole thing on video. Even if they weren't, would a call in from Richard appear later on a printout on my bed? I decided not to worry about it. This was irresistible, the name pulsing from the small silver device. *Richard*. I picked up.

"Hello?"

"Hi there," he said, the sweet, familiar voice, as if we had just seen each other the day before, over envelopes, and this was nothing out of the blue. "Am I catching you at a bad time?"

"Not exactly." My husband lost his job, he found the note that you wrote for me, and I'm sitting at home sipping wine contemplating the jealous frenzy he'll visit on me once he sees that you've called. But otherwise—it's a *great* time.

"I'll keep it brief," Richard said briskly. He always had been good at hearing my thoughts, even when I didn't speak them aloud. "I just—I need to see you. I'd like to see you. Is that possible? Tomorrow, say?"

My heart started its thudding again. Really, much as I adored Richard in the peculiar way that I did, it was hard to believe the relationship was the best thing for my organs. Too much pumping of blood, and the tendency toward arrhythmia. "Well—" I started to reply. He wanted to see me; I wanted to see him, too. I heard my husband's key in the door. "I'll call you," I said hastily, then shut the silver device and flung it some distance from me, as if it were a hot potato. My fingers were burning.

"Hi, sweetheart," I stood and said casually, natural as anything. "How was Mike?"

He came toward me, my husband, still lean and still handsome. A bit bony around the edges, but there was nothing so terrible about that. Once again his face had the weight on it of a Scotch or two, whatever they'd been drinking. And mine, to be fair, probably showed the slow slide of Chardonnay.

But sometimes these enhanced encounters don't go the way they do in the melodramas. Sometimes they're fine. Sodden, but fine.

"I love you, you know," my husband said heavily, leaning in to embrace me. I could feel it in him, through him: his love, his fear, his embarrassment. The poor man's confidence, this I understood, had taken a battering. "I want things to be good between us. I really love you. I'll do whatever it takes."

"I love you, too," I murmured, half holding him up, and this was not a lie, or a line. I did love this man I had married. In spite of the dishes, the television, the meter maids. I knew who he was under there, that sturdy, good-natured punster. I hated to see him torn up. I wanted to unbatter him, raise up his self-esteem. I wanted his arms to feel strong again: they could be so kind, when they were strong. I had made promises to and about this man, in a room full of people that included my mother, and I had always intended, and still did, to keep them. "I love you, too," I repeated, to make sure he heard.

But the human heart—what else can you say?—has its mysteries, its paradoxes. If I went back to my dictionary one day, I would have to address this: the many contradictory chambers you can have within one and the same heart. There was nothing insincere in what I said to my husband that night; nor was my embrace of him in any way false, some act to deceive him, nor, when we fell into bed together, was I obliging him merely for the sake of obliging him. My sighs were real. There was pleasure in our coupling for me, too. Though none more, perhaps, than when he had fallen asleep directly afterward, next to me, and soon was emitting the sounds of deep post-coital oblivion.

And that's when my imagination, sly fox that it was, crept back to Richard, and I wondered if I could work out some way to see him.

Ferry Boat

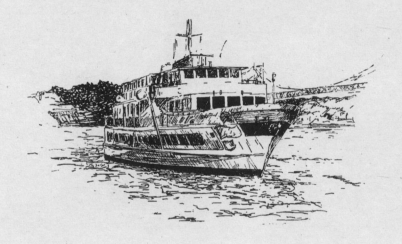

Fresh air — Cures many ills, and feels better than remaining in a compromised interior; but that doesn't mean that what you're doing out under the open skies is right.

⟶

The doorbell rang at an ungodly hour the next morning.

Here are some ways you can be rousted from a deep sleep: rosy-fingered dawn can tap gently on your eyelids—this in the days soon after you are married—and you can open your eyes to the possibility of renewed embraces with the amorous man lying next to you (assuming his young children aren't in the other room, having stayed overnight, in which case, lust or no lust, you'll feel too damned self-conscious); or you can be a kid, visiting your uncle who has a golden retriever named Special K, who comes over to you on the spare couch where you are and starts licking your face with dog-chowy breath, so you have to sit up and wipe the slobber off with your sleeve; or it can be the days before you have even met your future husband, when you are living in a city, and there's a delivery truck outside, some guy who starts thundering his big motor awake every morning in the darkness and thinks nothing of casting mariachi music out into the pre-dawn air, as he pulls away to make whatever deliveries he has to. And though you hear him and his engine and his mariachi music morning after morning, you never find a way to sleep through it, and so the man, whoever he is, has a permanent, intimate role in changing your sleep cycle.

Or it can be the ex-wife at the door ringing the doorbell insistently, with an impatient rhythm that somehow falls neatly in with that of your own nascent, throbbing headache.

"What the hell—?" my husband said next to me. I bet his head was pounding too. He tossed off the covers in annoyance—but not before leaning over to give my hair a kiss. That was sweet. That was the old husband for a minute. "All *right*! Jesus Christ! I'm *coming*!" he bellowed. That was more the husband I was used to. He got up and padded down to the door.

I crept over to the window, and looked out to see Ryan and Alan waiting forlornly in the van. Seeing them (they didn't see me) I felt a pang, something indescribable in an unknown corner of my interior. Those kids. Those boys.

"Well, it has to be here," I could hear Theresa hissing. It was January, a new year. Had the woman not made any resolutions at all? Something along the lines of *I will cease my shrewish ways*? Any pledge of that kind? "*I* don't have it. And he needs it for the field trip. They specifically instructed the kids to bring something warm, like down, because the ferryboat ride will be cold. The fog won't have lifted."

"So come in and take a look for yourself," my husband said. This was a kind of taunt on my husband's part. Ever since the tearing-photos-off-the-wall incident, DDT had stuck by her policy of not crossing our threshold. We had cooties, or germs, or perhaps we just had living proof that ours was a household like anyone else's. It might have distressed Theresa beyond repair to know that we did not inhabit a literal den of sin and depravity. There were Cheerios here, too. Lego. Monopoly. We were regular people, and her boys made their sometime home here, and this was not something she could allow herself to be aware of.

"I can't," I heard her say. "You know that."

"If it's so important to you to get the damn coat, come and get it." His footsteps headed toward the kitchen, source of caffeine and aspirin. The door was left open.

I got dressed quickly in something basic, jeans and a sweatshirt, in case I had to make an appearance. Generally speaking that would make things worse—seeing me was, for Theresa, like encountering the ghost of marriages past, and rendered her quivering and furious—but I felt I ought to be prepared. I looked out of the window again. The boys were still in the van. Still forlorn.

"He needs it for his *field* trip," the voice repeated loudly, as though the only problem to be overcome here was my husband's hardness of hearing. "We've got to get going. The bus leaves early from the school. Don't you—" OK, here it came, "don't you care about your son's well-being?"

"Don't I *care*?" my husband hollered. Even without coffee, yet, he could manage a pretty good holler. He was going on the adrenaline of hatred at this point. I'll say one thing for Theresa: she knew how to rile him. That's something you pick up after you've been married to someone, I guess. "Don't I *care*? What are you saying to me, after everything I've done for those boys? In spite of every goddamn roadblock you've tried to put in my way?"

I saw the children squirm in the car, getting the gist, if not, I hoped to God, the actual words. Then one boy said something to the other, there was a short conversation. I could see Ryan's face more clearly of the two. It was glum.

"Roadblocks?" The familiar sneer of the righteous. "I have just had to manage the best I can through all of this, as a single mother in an extremely painful and difficult—"

"Don't give me that single mother crap. These boys have a father. They have a *stepmother*. You are not the only—"

"Don't you fucking dare talk to me about *her*!"

That did it. One of them, the one that had drawn the short straw—Ryan, of course—got out of the van.

"Mom?" I saw more than heard. "Can we go? I'm going to be late for the field trip. It's OK, someone'll have a jacket I can borrow."

"*Just wait in the goddamn van!*" She had this in her, Mother Theresa. Her voice could wither what it touched. I saw Ryan shrink back. "Your father is making this very difficult. He's—"

"I'm not doing a fucking thing. I'm telling you to come in and get the coat, if you need it. It will not kill you to come into this condo."

I shivered, in the air's cold and its poison. I reached for my husband's jacket, hanging on the doorknob of our room, and put it on. I shoved my hands deep in his pockets and felt the car keys nestling there, metal unlockers of speed and escape.

"What is this, some sick power play on your part? What are you *doing* to me here?"

"I'm not doing anything. I am just tired of you conveying to our children the idea that this house is somehow infected to the point where you cannot even set foot in here. They *see* this; they *see* you."

"Mom?" I could hear Ryan now.

"Just a *minute!*" Theresa hurled at him, as if the word were a blade, and at that moment something in me snapped. The ability, maybe, to sit still and watch these two adults enact this horror before their offspring. I didn't mind, I have to admit, my husband letting DDT have it—I suppose I haven't been able fully to disguise my lack of friendly feeling toward the woman—but not in front of the boys. For God's sake. Wasn't that Rule Number One, right at the beginning of the divorce manual? *Not in front of the children.*

I managed to get out of the condo and past the venom-spewer safely. The element of surprise was in my favor. A moment later I was on the sidewalk, opening my husband's car, saying, with what calm I could muster, "Come on, guys. I'll take you. Your mom and dad have some things to work out. Why don't you hop in."

And then Theresa was torn, because to prevent this action would mean having to acknowledge me, something she was religiously disinclined to do. Her eyes widened in dismay as the boys stood on the sidewalk, hesitating; and then their father stepped in with admirable paternal authority, saying from the doorway, "That's a good idea—Alan, Ryan, why don't you get in with Pan and go to school. Your mother and I have to talk here for a few minutes."

Or scream, or inflict machete wounds, or however you want to put it. Still, the survivalist instinct that is quite strong in kids trumped what remaining pull of loyalty they felt toward their mother, and with alacrity they moved over into their dad's car.

"Bye, Mom," said Alan, taking charge, as the male head of their household. "Will you pick us up at the regular time?"

"Yes," Theresa replied, subdued. "I'll be there." Her venom was all but gone and she was on the brink, I could see through the car window, of tears. Oh, and then my husband would comfort her, that's how that would go. She would finally eke pity out of him, and that was why she was willing to let me, the horned devil, drive away with her boys. Six years later, she was still holding on. There was no letting go.

"You'd better step on it, Pan," Alan said, strapping himself in. "The kid doesn't want to miss his field trip." As the older brother, Alan took native pleasure in referring to Ryan as "the kid." Usually he did it to get a rise out of his junior, but this morning the tease fell on ears tired already of what they had had to hear, and Ryan did not reply.

As the doors closed on the car, there was a small collective sigh of relief that we were leaving that messy pile of entrails behind. None of us would acknowledge it openly, but it gave the air in the car a certain camaraderie.

"So where is this field trip to?" I asked the face in the rearview mirror. I was aiming for a perky, that-never-happened tone, but I could see that Ryan looked bitten and bruised.

"To the city," he said. "We're going to some maritime museum. On the ferryboat."

"You're taking a ferryboat to get there?"

He nodded. "We're doing a unit on transportation."

"How exciting!" I was thinking of high winds and rocky waters, and the fact that he would certainly need, as his mother had said, something warmer to wear than his thin T-shirt.

"But I'm going to miss it." He was gloomy. "The buses leave from the school early. By eight."

"You won't miss it—we'll get you there. Pan Limousine Services makes that commitment to you."

A half smile from Alan only, who said, "I don't know—the kid is nervous. The kid thinks he's going to get left behind and have to spend all day in the library with Ms. Rubin, who has bad breath."

"Shut up."

"But still likes to call him Sweetheart, because she has a soft spot for this kid that dates back to the time—"

"Shut *up*."

"Now, fellas . . ." I was driving as fast as I could so that I wouldn't have to listen to them bicker, as well as for the more obvious reason. We were there soonish, and I almost got us all killed only once or twice. Alan, now in middle school, got let off first, so at least we could deposit preteen sarcasm on the sidewalk before seeing how the field-trip cliffhanger would resolve. "Bye, kid," Alan said as he got out, to which his brother replied with a rude gesture I won't try to transcribe here. "Whatever you do, don't get seasick. You don't want to have to look at all that ketchup and eggs coming back up."

"Thank you, Alan," I said conclusively, but it was as that last joke faded away that I looked toward the street ahead and could see that the stretch in front of the lower school—not good semantically, incidentally, for a younger brother to have to refer to his school as "lower"—was sickeningly empty. Ryan noticed this at the same time. "They left already," he said in a mouse-small voice of resignation. "We missed them."

"Maybe the buses haven't arrived yet. Maybe we're early." I felt like a surgeon holding out fake hopes for a miracle.

"No." He shook his head heavily, his lips pushed forward in youthful despair. "Ms. Astor kept telling us we had to get here early. She kept *telling* us." His eyes puddled with disappointment.

Well, I couldn't let that happen. This poor boy, who had already this morning witnessed the gross corpse of his parents' marriage laid out for him yet again (and how could you kill something over and over? how could they keep having to kill something that was supposedly already dead?)—I couldn't consign this boy to a day in the library with the noisome Ms. Rubin. I had to help.

"I'll take you there myself." I pulled away from the school.

"Take me where?"

"To the ferry terminal. I know where they leave from. We'll find your group. We'll catch up with them." This would make me late for Mr. Finkelstein, which had never happened before in five years, but I considered myself in an emergency. I could use my handy silver device to let him know. That's what I had it for.

At which moment, having been thought about, the device itself rang. It was my husband. Calling me up to debrief.

"Jesus *Christ*," he started. Not Him again. Why drag Jesus Christ into everything? Surely He had better things to think about. "Unbelievable. Unfuckingbelievable."

"I've got Ryan in the car still," I told my husband, to stem the flow of expletives. Not that they were audible, I hoped, but my husband was not a quiet man, especially when offloading about his ex. "We missed the bus for the field trip, so I'm going to drive him directly to the ferry terminal and try to catch up with the school group there."

"The *ferry* terminal?"

"They're going to the city on the ferryboat."

"Ah." He scarcely registered it. "Anyway, so after you left, I told her I wasn't going to be able to make the payments anymore, because—Oh, hold on, that's her trying on the other line. What does she want *now*. She's probably calling to apologize. She was such a—Hold on. Let me see what she wants."

Or, I thought into the phone, you could not pick up when she calls. Or you could spare me the details. Or you could make a conversation with me, your wife, appear more important, for once, than a furthering of hostilities, or reconciliations, with the plaid living-room set you cohabited with the first time.

I closed the phone. Who needs to wait on hold with their own husband? Nobody. When I need to wait on hold, I'll call the phone company. They're the pros.

"So—the maritime museum?" I chirped to the small face in the mirror. "That'll be fun!"

The phone toodled again, and I opened it with a "Yes?" of impatience. Really, I was about to let my husband have it, after this morning we'd been through.

"Hello, Angel."

My heart stopped. But only for a second. Then it remembered that it had better keep beating if I was safely to get this boy to his ferryboat.

"Hi," I breathed.

"Is this a bad time?"

"Oh—" I laughed, actually. "Well, it's—we're—" How to begin? I wanted to tell Richard everything. *Everything*. I wanted to fall into his arms. "I'm glad you called."

"I've been missing you, Angel." His voice still had that warmth, that solidity, that I loved and wanted to lean into, but there was a sadness that crackled through it, too. I was pretty sure that was in him and not on the phone line.

"Me, too," I said, pressing the phone closer to my ear, as if I could pull the man somehow into my brain, to keep me company in there, with all the rest of the racket.

"Are you on your way to work?" he asked. "Don't worry, I know I'd better not show up there."

"I'm driving, actually. I'm taking Ryan—he was supposed to go on a field trip today, and we missed the school bus, so I'm taking him down to the ferry terminal to try to catch the group there."

"The ferry terminal? I love ferryboats." There he was again, my Richard! My big, sandy-voiced Richard—his enthusiasm, his optimism, intact. What a gift that was. "How about if I meet you there?"

"At the—at the—"

"Sure!" Easiest thing in the world, he made it sound. Why not? Who knew where he was, how far he was coming from? Didn't matter! Why not meet me at the ferry terminal? Would my husband find out? Not a problem! Let's worry about that later. "At the ferry terminal. I'll see you there. I'll be the one with the pink carnation."

"I—well, you know—"

There were so many surges within me: of fear, of guilt, of desire. Here it was January, a new year, and I hadn't seen Richard since the Thanksgiving park bench, and I wanted to with a ferocity that was clawing at me from inside, like a frantic beast trying to get out of its cage. I had no idea how to tame this, how to stay steady.

"OK," I said simply. That was the easiest thing to say. The pink-carnation joke, terrible as it was, somehow clinched it. "Sounds good." I closed the phone and placed it gently on the empty passenger seat beside me, where in a moment another toodle came from its silver shape. How wearisome these devices were; how impossible they made it to have a single thought for yourself. One instant of reflection.

"We're pulling up to the ferry terminal now," I informed the guy on the other end of the line. I had assumed, correctly this time, that it was my spouse. "I'll call you back." I hardly gave him time to grunt his assent. Then I decided, defiantly, to turn off the phone before closing it. Its toodles were tiring me.

The thing was, *terminal* was a little grand, as a word, to capture where we were. We were in a parking lot with a coffee and hot dog stand, near a small jetty that led to some brownish water, at the end of which was a small shelter and a sign posted with some schedules. It was a liquid bus stop, really, no more. And it was deserted. I found a fleecy garment of my husband's lying on the passenger seat next to me and handed it to Ryan, who put it on wordlessly. It would make him look something like a street urchin, but at least he wouldn't get hypothermia. Ryan and I got out of the car. He stood with his backpack on over the long, droopy sweatshirt, looking lost.

"We've missed them." He was morose. "They've gone already."

"Well, wait a second now." The place was a ghost town, admittedly. On the street nearby was a sprawling bedding-supply store and a cheap-imports-made-by-slave-labor emporium. The coffee/hot dog stand sold muffins the size of cantaloupes, wrapped tightly in plastic, and donuts encrusted with a sugary glaze that looked like it would rot your teeth immediately on impact. "Let me check the schedule," I said to Ryan. "Maybe there will be another one that we could catch, and then—"

"No, no. Forget it. We missed them. It's too late."

I had to be strong here, so I went over to peer at the posting by the shelter while Ryan waited droopily in the lot. There would be another boat, yes, in forty minutes. Forty minutes in this ghost town, or a lifetime: which was longer? When I turned back there was at least a new sign of humanity other than Ryan and me, a large man purchasing something at the coffee/hot dog stand. The man turned, holding a wrapped raisin-bran cantaloupe and the cavity-inducing sugar glaze.

It was Richard.

Where had he come from? Had he driven there? In what? The man was like Mary Poppins, blowing in on an umbrella. He was dressed casually, for him: no tight-fitting suit today, rather a pair of dark slacks—I had the impression Richard wasn't a blue-jeans guy—and a nicely Arctic-looking dark-red parka that enveloped him like a sleeping bag. He looked as though he were about to go study penguin and elephant-seal populations. (The sky was now clearing and the sun began to assert itself, as it does so often in our state, but the January air still had a cool morning shiver, a bayside bite.) Richard's green eyes were alight and his pale skin looked strangely undernourished, but he was animated all over with pleasure at seeing me.

My body turned loose on seeing him, too: my bones became bendy and my knees went about weakening, and my hands shook until I tucked them under my arms to still them. "Hi there," I called to my fellow, my friend. My face felt like a Sunkist orange, sliced open into a crescent smile of sweetness. "How are you?" I wanted to throw an embrace around him, hidden though he was in his sleeping bag of a jacket. It was a desire I tried to convey subtly, with the sparkle in my eyes and the husk in my voice.

"Good!" he beamed, bright as a thousand-watt flashlight. "Even better, now." He walked toward us brandishing his two food items, as though their weights were helping him keep his balance.

Ryan was watching this encounter with the wide, absorbing gaze of a ten-year-old, not afraid to stare. His nose ran in the cold and he wiped it unthinkingly on his sleeve. To Richard's amiable "And you must be Ryan," the boy simply nodded, as if this were a lucky guess. If he had been Alan, he would have demanded bluntly, "Who are you?" But Ryan was a kid who let silence do a lot of the work for him. That was something I liked about him. "I'm Richard," Richard supplied into the empty space provided, and Ryan nodded at that too, like there was no surprise there. "I'd shake your hand, but both of mine are loaded with carbohydrates."

Ryan smiled faintly at that, a smile that firmed up when Richard held the two hands out in a gesture of surrender. "I can't eat both of these, Ryan—look at me—I have enough heft already. Do me a favor and take one of them."

"Can I have the donut?" he asked, looking at Richard, not me, because he knew what I'd say.

"Of course! An excellent choice." Richard forked over the monstrous glazed ring to Ryan, whose eyes drooled with anticipation. Really, sugar can in its evil way bring such immediate delight to a person. "In my experience, there are very few problems," Richard offered, echoing my thoughts, "that a donut can't solve." So much for my years of puritan nutritional cheerleading. But Richard was right, in that the donut seemed to give Ryan strength and resolve for the morning. When Richard said a few minutes later, "So, we've got a boat to wait for, is that right, to catch up with the rest of your posse?" Ryan nodded, abandoning his earlier defeatism, and when Richard suggested we sit over on the jetty and play cards till the boat came, Ryan nodded agreeably, his mouth full of glaze and gummy donut dough. And when we all three sat, cross-legged, near the boat stop, Richard handily pulled a deck of cards like a rabbit from the folds of his big red coat, and Ryan watched with interest as Richard started dealing us seven cards each.

"So, Ryan—do you know how to play poker?" he asked. Ryan shook his head and Richard got down to explaining, while Ryan, donut-sated, listened carefully, as though poker were a crucial unit being covered in today's class and he'd better pay attention so that he'd score well on the test.

By the time the ferryboat chugged into view on the choppy bay, we were well into seven-card stud, Ryan having accumulated a significant portion of the paperclips we were betting with. He was a quick learner. Richard told him that when we got onto our boat we'd start to play with real money, so loading onto the gleaming small vessel was drained of its seafaring drama, and became simply a transition to a more comfortable poker salon. I paid for our tickets and the three of us sat down together at a table inside and resumed playing cards, as if this were something we did every day—ride the ferryboat, betting paperclips and pennies provided by Richard, not bothered by the dip and rise as the boat took on the frosted waves, protected as we were, inside, from the abrasions of the bay's salty wind. If Ryan was still worried about seasickness or the whereabouts of his classmates, he didn't show it. To look at him you'd guess he'd be perfectly happy to hang out with Richard all day, trying to gamble his way into a fortune.

About halfway through the crossing I excused myself from the game and just sat with the light and the air and the motion, letting the morning's sensations catch up with me. Here I was, crossing the bay on a ferry, violating all kinds of rules. I had not even called Finkelstein to tell him I wouldn't be in that morning, which was unheard of, my absence and irresponsibility, both. Yet, in spite of the violation, and the rocking of the boat, internally I felt strangely calm and unruffled. There would be consequences to this adventure, doubtless. We would get Ryan reunited, so I hoped, with his clan, but after that would follow the blunt reality of Richard and me alone together, and somewhere beyond that a husband of mine none too pleased with the development. At the base of my stomach was a heavy lining of dread at that thought. But here and now, in the present—and Richard had always exhorted me to *live in the present*, in his winning seventies' inflection, not to *feel regret for the past* or *fear for the future*—I was simply happy, here on this boat with these two guys, my friend and my stepson. It was something I had been, all my life, innately suspicious of— the *now*, I mean—but here on this day, in this morning air, I was willing to give the place a try. Because the *then* of my husband and Theresa screaming in front of the children had been so wrenching and so terrible, and the *what's next* of my husband's likely explosive discovery of this outing was appalling enough that it didn't bear to be thought of. I watched gulls cut diagonal patterns across the sky and listened to Richard and Ryan sharing casual card talk, and I inhaled a vision that had more horizon in it than I was used to in my short-circuited life. I felt the thrum of the engines beneath me and for a moment it all made sense and was unified, part of one, indivisible whole. The *now*. This must be what Richard meant. It was a great feeling.

I closed my eyes briefly as if to shutter the moment, like a camera snap, so I would never forget it, whatever came next. But I suppose closing my eyes was a way to step back from it, too, because my then-tending mind immediately supplied other images, took me off somewhere else. To Millie and me playing gin rummy for hours at the kitchen table together, when I was a kid. Eating crackers and drinking milk (Millie drank buttermilk, a revolting substance in my opinion but there was no accounting for grownups' predilections)—Millie saying, if she had a good hand, "One two three four five six seven eight nine ten! Who's excited? I'm not excited!" or sighing, with pretend heaviness, "Oh, dear . . . If I was married, I wouldn't be here," if the cards hadn't gone her way. Millie was married, but to a brute who didn't deserve her. If you knew her, if you loved her, if you played rummy and ate snacks with her, you wanted for Millie a prince, because only a prince would be good enough.

"We're here," a gentle voice said, and there was a touch on my arm. I opened my eyes to Richard's kindness, and could feel the engines slowing beneath us. The ferry was arriving at a dock in the city. I shook myself into alertness. As we made our way off the boat a ferry functionary said, "Would your son like a sticker?" handing me a company decal, and the notion that Ryan might be my son, that the three of us might be seen as a family, left me speechless for a moment. It had occasionally happened before, of course, with the boys, that a waitress or bowling alley operative might call me their mom, but when Alan was around there was always a loud disavowal: "She's not our mother!" In this case it was Richard who said cheerfully, "Sure!" taking the sticker, and if it bothered Ryan at all to be associated with two people not his blood relatives, he did not let on. When Richard slapped the decal on his backpack, saying, "Here you go, Sport—to commemorate the day you wiped me clean out of paperclips," Ryan grinned with sweet pride. *He's a good kid*, I could imagine Richard telling me later, and, looking at the brave, dark-haired boy, I thought to myself that Ryan was truly that. A good kid.

Happily the maritime museum was there near the dock, and it was surprisingly easy to go in and find an excitable batch of fifth-graders wreaking their havoc. There was something touching about watching Ryan go. The minute he saw his classmates he dissolved among them like a sugar cube in a cup of tea, and it was immediately impossible to distinguish him from the others. "Goodbye" was a matter of a nod and a low, near-imperceptible wave, and in my forward-looking way I suddenly saw him as a kid starting college, eager to shed an unwanted connection with the people who had tried haplessly to raise him. (In my experience, when divorce tears your family up, from that point on all there is to look forward to is the neutrality of college.) I had a brief parental-type encounter with Ryan's teacher confirming the hand off and then we were released, Richard and I, back into the atmosphere. We did not linger in the museum with its model freighters and its lifesavers. We both tacitly realized the boy wanted us gone.

Outside, we wandered bayside for a bit, in silence. Skyscrapers loomed at some distance, cars conveyed noxious noises and emissions, tourists busied the broad sidewalks with their maps and their languages. Now that Ryan was gone, a crucial distraction for Richard and me was missing. We no longer had a purpose being where we were. This was just the two of us now, a woman and a man not her husband, together in the shiny, anonymous city, and I started to feel a flutter of panic in my stomach. There were too many possibilities here. The city was big, full and frightening. Plenty of people, famously, lost their morals right here, or if not here precisely then in theres very near by.

I began to think I should probably head home. The explosion was waiting for me. I might as well go back to it and get myself blown up.

"Look—another ferry." Richard pointed to a blue-and-gold sign we had come upon. "Going the other way—to the town by the mountain. I've always wanted to go there." He said it mildly, like a child asking for a second cupcake, knowing you'll say no. Richard could, I guessed, feel the vibration of anxiety within me now. He was not going to push me.

But the mountain. The town. All that had happened there that had led to my Dictionary. I had not been back since before everything—before my husband and I had met, married, and managed whatever it was exactly we had managed together. The town by the mountain. I had imagined, hadn't I, once?—that Richard might have his home there. Now he was telling me he had never been.

"Shall we go?" I asked softly. My heart hammered as I asked him. How far off the pier was I planning to walk with this man? What would I tell my husband when he finally caught up with me?

"I'd love to," Richard said, his face bathed in sun and affection. "I'd like nothing better." He put a padded arm around my shoulders—he was still wearing his sleeping bag—as we made our way to the ticket booth, and like so much about Richard, the gesture had an ambiguity about it. His arm was loose and floppy, and it might have been expressing nothing more than *my old buddy, my old pal—let's hop on this boat together, just for a ride*. Though my husband would no doubt bludgeon the man to death were he there to see it, I could tell myself that, really, appearances notwithstanding, the whole thing was perfectly innocent. I was just traveling, with my friend, to a geography that had once had significance for me. That was all I was doing.

On the other hand, staying with honesty for a moment, aiming at full disclosure . . . When Richard and I stepped on board the ferryboat together, and his hand reached for mine, I had the distinct, unambiguous sensation that this was a parallel world we had just moved over to, the kind Richard liked to read about in his favorite science-fiction novels, where he was free, and I was. Where there were no ex-wives or stepsons and there was no angry, distraught husband. The past was clean, pure, and empty, the future a blank canvas, so there was nothing wrong with our fondness or desire for one another, and here we were, the two of us, setting forth on our honeymoon.

The Mountain

Zen — You may find lines of Zen-like philosophy mysteriously seductive coming from someone you don't know very well. Strangely enough, you may also find they contain an element of truth.

—⊸—

Another boat, another crossing.

The sun seemed to fall down on us in a syncopated rhythm that echoed the chop of the waves, and when we got past all the clutter and urbanity of the city we were opened up to a clear view of the graceful orange bridge that we Westerners, in our grandiosity, like to call golden. (As any local will tell you, it's really a paint color called International Orange, a name that reflects the city's global aspirations.)

"Look at that," Richard said. We were standing out on the deck of the boat, and his body was close to mine though we were not holding hands. *Substantial*, I'd called him to my husband, and he was; he was a comfort, he was solid, he gave the sense that his presence was something you could count on. I leaned in toward him, for support. "It is beautiful here," he murmured. "Isn't it?"

If I had listened more keenly, I might have heard the wistfulness in Richard's voice, the anticipation of loss; I might have had an idea of why we were spending this day together. But all I heard was the remark. It made him sound like a foreigner, somehow, impressed by what we'd managed to come up with here with our hills and our water, and our famous bridge. I responded with the native's casual pride: Well yes it is, it is beautiful, in spite of our freeways and our toll plazas (who thought of calling such godforsaken stretches *plazas?*), our exhausted, commuter-filled air, our helpless crowding and greed—we haven't managed to wreck it entirely, we've tried to keep the area nice so that visitors like you can enjoy it. For people who grew up here, as I did, its beauties and glories are sunk so far within us that we can keep seeing the orchards even when they've been cleared to make room for Italianate villas, we can draw the sweep of the bay in the palms of our hands, and dinosaur-sized redwoods haunt the unremembered corners of our dreams. The notorious fog—the region's winter-scented, creaturely, dusk-and-dawn fog—never altogether lifts. This place is inside us, no matter what else happens.

Being back on the water returned me to that truth. It also pulled my attention away from this curious revelation: that when a longed-for event opens up in front of you, it can be difficult to know what is happening or how to enjoy it. Standing next to Richard on this blue-and-gold boat, gulping down life and liberty on this, our all-too-short pursuit of happiness, I felt a little like my old dog when he used to get wet in the fall rains and would start running in mad muddy circles around the garden, chasing some unreal squirrel or rabbit. It was as though the downpour of water made him so excited he didn't even know where he was anymore. I was the same with Richard. How often had I imagined being somewhere safe, away from everyone and everything else, with this man, so that at last I could have all the conversations with him I'd dreamed of? How deeply had I missed having around me my bearded, full-bodied direct line to the universe and its workings, who might help interpret for me its mysterious patterns and challenges? I hadn't seen my friend Richard (well, again, *friend*) in so many weeks—since the long winter school break and its attendant scheduling mayhem with the children, since a job loss and a Puffin session and a Christmas that was not, on balance, one of the elves' finest. I had so much to tell Richard. There was a husband to describe, all that shouting and grief, the stubble and the drunkenness (if mild). I had so much to say, to ask, to work out. Where to start? How to jump in?

I ended up talking about Millie.

I wanted to give Richard my story. Not every detail, not every childish episode: I left out camping on the hillside with my best friends the Chen girls, that long summer evening when we played fierce games of Sorry and snacked from a cold chest full of pickles, salami, and oranges; I skipped horseback-riding along the wooded path alone, as a teenager, when I was thrown or I fell and had my shocking, existential moment of body-thudding ignominy; I omitted the fights in high school with my mother over the accented boy who wanted to kiss me and whose attentions filled my cautious, pale mom with alarm. (Somewhere embedded in that tale was an entry for my Dictionary of Betrayal, if I could only work out its shape.) Richard and I didn't have time for all that—it was only one bay we were crossing—so instead I stuck with what seemed essential. And at that moment, it was Millie. Of the infinite bouquet of memories and conundrums to choose from, my bewildered butterfly mind settled on Millie.

She was wonderful and benevolent, our old neighbor. She helped raise me, really, given the strains my mother was under (without a husband around, after a nasty, soul-splitting divorce of her own—well, it's a long story; they all are). Millie took the dog for walks with me and she taught me to play gin rummy, of course, and also how to make mouthwatering chocolate-chip cookies, the latter a skill that came in handy years later with the two boys who were, on particular days of the week, in my care. Millie often came over in the afternoons when my Mom was out working, and on our ratty old couch we watched hours of game shows together, those television vapidities intended to destroy the brain and its workings, though the uncanny companionship produced by watching game shows with someone is, in its way, unique. I loved Millie, which Richard could tell from the stories I poured out to him about her as we stood rocking over the salted waves, weaving near sailboats, swallowing the fresh, noisy air. And though Richard could not know where these stories were leading, I did. I knew.

I suppose I understood, and Richard did, that one reason I was telling him about Millie now was not just that I missed her keenly, her unshakeable good, her deep, rooted affection—not to mention her humor—but that he, Richard, struck me as having many of the same qualities. He made me feel as Millie once had, not just that life was bearable but that I myself was redeemable, something that the thick, inescapable murk of the Theresa years had made me doubt.

As I told Richard my Millie stories, the ferryboat continued its journey, and the mountain itself hove into view. (And don't you love that word, *hove*, that just sits around waiting for its rare appearances, like the orchestra's wood block or triangle, perpetually quiet save for its proud instant of importance?) That particular mountain, if you don't know it, has not only the most lyrical double iamb of a name but also suggests peace, old times, contemplation. It stands as a cool, dark-green challenge to the frantic materialism that busies itself at its base. Its head is often in the clouds, or the fog sits low and clings to the bay, and the mountain rises above it, its peak visible over the ghostly gray. People walk up it and round it, of course, for exercise and self-betterment, and there are those who have married, barefoot, in meadows near its summit, but you can also take its lessons from a distance, you can listen to it and watch it from a house, or a car, or a boat.

"Millie lived there," I told Richard. "In the shadow of that mountain."

He nodded. "What a place to be." His tone had some awe in it, which was appropriate, and his eyes were a deep, appreciative green, but again there was an ellipsis there, an unprovided end of sentence that if I'd been paying closer attention I would have asked him to supply. Richard had something significant to tell me, and I had not noticed, so concerned was I with foraging in my own past. (Neither had I paid attention to the silver device in my pocket, which must contain within it message upon message from the other side of the water, no doubt exhorting me, in a different sort of tone, to pay attention to the *now*.)

The ferryboat deposited us at a landing, from where we could take a bus into town. A destination had by now taken shape in my head, and so insistent was this destination that it all but silenced the rest: my love for Richard, the wrongness of my love for Richard, my love for my husband, my memory of that awful pre-breakfast scene with DDT and the boys, my submerged awareness that there must be threats and entreaties condensed into my cell phone's tiny memory chip, somewhere, however the hell that worked. As Richard and I sat side by plastic-seated side on a bus populated by hapless tourists and solemn domestic employees and no one much in between, I had that fleeting sense of criminality you tend to get—in this state, at least—when you find yourself carless, as I watched nondescript housing-industry sprawl roll past us (flooring and appliance warehouses, second-home-furniture suppliers). Once again Richard reached for my hand, and I readily yielded it to his soft-fleshed clasp, feeling a furtive thrill and a guilt and a quandary. I still could not read him. The hand-holding was either that of a companion who will never leave you no matter how dingy the bus, how rough the going, or that of a friendly large fellow who can sense that you're becoming slightly unhinged. When I said to him, "I have an idea of where we could go," Richard smiled at me and replied calmly, "Then let's go there."

We got off at the back of the town, finally, where latte-dispensing cafés and colorful trinketerías gave shaded way to what passed in this place for a public park. The park did not, in itself, look promising—with that great mountain looming over-head, any ordinary park could only seem dwarf-like and foolish—but it led, as I knew from the days that predated my dictionary, up through damp, park-bench-edged lawns (more inviting for drug

deals than canoodling) into the cemetery. A place, like the stationery store, all too easy to misspell. And that's where I took us:
into the cemetery.

We walked along quiet, uneven paths that wove in and around
the many silent deceased, and then, under the dark arms of a
Cyprus tree, Richard suddenly stopped.

"Let's pause here for a moment," he said.

This was not, just yet, my destination, but I paused obligingly.

"You're smart to find this place," Richard commented. "There's
nobody else here." And it dawned on me then, in blushing, rosy-
fingered fashion, that we did not, my friend and I, have the same
thing in mind at that moment. Unsurprisingly. He may have been
Santa Claus, my dear, sleeping-bagged Richard, but he did not
know what I wanted, exactly.

He turned my shoulders gently so I faced him, and now, in this
cool, morbid light I did at last see the look in his green eyes I had
never been sure of before. Lust. You can't mistake it, when you see
it. It luminates like nothing else.

"You're so pretty, Angel," Richard said to me, stroking my
cheek with his thumb, and that was when I recognized that something within me had changed. Because unlike the first instance of
that gesture, one warm falafel afternoon, when I had swooned at
Richard's touch, now I felt my eyes dip shyly, and my whole self
want to move slightly, inoffensively, out of the way. I was not
ready for this. This was not, after all, where my heart was.

"Thank you," I said with the sideways smile, the elsewhere look.

"Here," Richard murmured, and he leaned forward into what
was clearly meant to be a kiss.

I diverted it. Here was Richard's mouth moving toward mine, that meeting I had so often and so hungrily imagined, and here was I, dodging, in order to plant my lips somewhere different. On his ear. Near the sandy red hair, the sweaty, bristled neck. A place that can, in context, be one hot spot among many in a passionate engagement, but with this gentle peck was chosen to convey, wordlessly but clearly: *No thanks*.

"There's somewhere I want to go," I whispered to Richard (in lieu of an apology for the fact that I did not desire his lips on mine). "Someone I need to see."

He looked at me quizzically. The hunger had not left him. He had worked patiently toward this moment, and this moment was being denied him; and like anyone denied he wore a face of disappointment: clouded eyes, bitten lips. But what could good Richard, champion of Zen acceptance and accommodation, say but "OK"?

I led Richard up a further hill, through Pettits and Edmunds and around the occasional Lovelace, past headstones and cat sculptures and small block-lettered slabs implanted in the ground. It was a jumbled, friendly cemetery here, not one of those broad-boulevarded kinds you sometimes see for the wealthy that have street names and addresses and probably astronomical property taxes. This was more the humble-bouquets-in-vases variety, where the bereaved have left photos sealed up to protect against the seepings of the fog. I have always found cemeteries soothing; I like the sense of closure you find there. And sure enough, it was not long before we found the cold, apt place, a dove-gray marble rectangle inscribed with *Millicent Larsen*. This was my idea of our destination, Richard, I thought of saying, but he was getting it now. *Not lust.*

MILLICENT LARSEN. I liked the way Millie's full name seemed like a meeting of *militant* and *innocent*, which captured her fierce sweetness, her pure strength. I looked at her name on that stone and remembered the grace in her voice, the comfort in her presence. I recalled the blue hue of her eyes and her ability to make a joke out of nothing. And then I thought of all that had happened while she was still alive, and how I came to start writing my Dictionary of Betrayal. I remembered some of the entries: **Abandonment.** **Cheating. Self-deception. Neglect**: *Don't underestimate the significance of not telling a friend something you should have.* **Sex**: *Try not to have it with the wrong person, the wrong person, the wrong person.* I breathed in sharply and leaned close to Richard. Suddenly I felt weak.

MILLICENT LARSEN had been a real friend to my mother, the one who understood how broken my mother was after my father left her. **Divorce**: *It's a bastard.* I was no use at the time—I had just been born—but kind Millie was there to help pick up the pieces, to try to make my mom whole again. Long years later, when I had grown up, Millie was the only person I told about the child I chose not to have. She helped me find the clinic, and afterwards she made me hot cocoa and we watched some vapid game shows together, just like we used to. **Mistakes made when younger**: *They will haunt you, they will keep on haunting you.* I never even told my husband about that episode in my past: I did not want him to think less of me, stupid though that sounds now. Then somehow, by the time I might have told him, it seemed too late.

And yet, with all that, growing up alongside the jokes and games of gin rummy, when Millie eventually fell ill with that elder-killer, pneumonia, I did not make it back to her in time to say goodbye, to tell her once again that I loved her. It was shortly after my husband and I met and the whirlwind had started its whirling, and I thought there was more time for me to get there than there proved to be. She died before I could see her. That was unforgivable. Wasn't it? Certainly she was no longer around to forgive me. **Unsaid farewells**: *You should have been there. Whatever excuse you may have, the fact is you should have been there*. That, in the end, was the first entry I wrote, and it went on at some length.

I had thought to tell Richard this. I had thought to make to him a free and full confession, and I had imagined—what? Richard's great, salving absolution. "It's all right, Angel," Richard would console me. "You did the best that you could. You meant well." But I had drafted that imaginary script before Richard tried to kiss me. If there was something simple that attempted kiss had proved, it was that, in the end, Richard was a man. He was not Santa Claus, in spite of appearances. He was not Mary Poppins. His sweet, leaning-toward-me movement with a mouth full of lust had had the unintended effect on me of a slap in the face. It woke me up. *No*. This is not the man you want to hold. And no. This is not the man you have to tell. And no one, not even Richard, can bring back Millie, or anyone else that you've lost.

I finally did break down then. I suppose the tombs around there had seen such scenes often—I was only doing what people normally do in front of those cold stones. It was the familiar progression: you start weeping for the one you lost, and from there for the other losses you've had in your life, all the comings and goings, the passions that slowly turned into missed opportunities (and the missed opportunities that turned into passions), the griefs, the misplaced angers, the mistakes. Though Richard, bless him, did not believe in mistakes.

He held me while I wept, stroking my hair, but I felt the quaver in him: this was not the kind of holding he had hoped for. "Don't be sad, Angel. Don't be sad." Which was like telling the mountain to stop being a mountain. "It's all right," he soothed. "It's all right."

"How?" I shook my head, not sharing his optimism. "How can it be?" I wiped my face dry, tried to smear the tears off my cheeks. I can't have been pretty by then, sob stained as I was. Pink nosed and streamy eyed.

"It isn't all right," I said to Richard. "It's all wrong. It's all always been wrong. My husband and me being together, and Theresa hating us as she does, and those two doomed boys, and—"

"I liked Ryan," Richard offered. "He's a great kid. He has a lot of spirit."

"I knew you'd say that." But I said this with affection. "I think he liked you too. He seemed at ease with you." I sighed, remembering the family of three we had briefly been. Too bad the ferryboat had not been a cruise ship. We could have stayed on board for months, disembarking occasionally in colorful places like Sydney or Tokyo. I would have enjoyed a vacation of that kind.

"You'll do fine with those kids," Richard said confidently, and this time I did notice something—the future tense. He was making predictions now. My Applebee oracle. And yet he was, implicitly, not part of the scene he was foreseeing. "I think you're better off than you realize. I could tell Ryan trusted you. He felt safe with you."

"He was eating a donut. That puts anyone in a good mood."

"Admittedly." There it was again, the Richard grin. Hadn't seen it in a while. "But I think you'll do fine with them," he repeated, "—really."

"But *Theresa*," I sighed. "You don't understand. Just this morning—"

"Theresa's unimportant."

"What?"

"Theresa's—" He waved a hand. "Theresa is the past. She's what's passed. You have to pay attention to the present."

Here it was again. The damned *now*. I wanted to be able to agree with him, but he didn't understand. "You don't understand. She—"

He raised a hand to shut me up. I shut up.

"Listen, Angel. What is important is you and your husband, now. You say things aren't all right. Do you want them to be? Would you like it to be all right between you?"

I paused over the question, wondering what Richard's motive was in asking me, whether he was laying a trap I would unwittingly fall into. But when I read that open, Irish-inflected face, with its green eyes and its lucky-clover mouth, I saw again what I had seen before in Richard. From the start. From the very first envelope. He had that diamond-rare quality of genuine, strings-free concern.

Real interest. I *mattered* to him. He was asking me a question, a substantial one, about my life. He was asking me to consider.

"Yes," I finally answered him, quietly. I was thinking of the lean, handsome man and the entwining we had shared, Chardonnay-enhanced, Scotch-fueled, the night before. (That was just the night before!) It had felt good, our entwining. I loved that man, after all. I hated him, certainly, for bringing Theresa to bear on my life, and I resented him for half a dozen domestic lacunae, and I could have done altogether without the meter-maid diatribes and the co-worker denouncements—but I did love that man. I wore his ring. I wanted good things for him. I wanted something like peace. "Yes," I affirmed, more definitely, to Richard. "I would like things to be all right. But—"

"Now, now!" Richard put his hand up again to shush me. He was a little like a preacher, or a teacher. Or a guru. My husband had always worried I'd be susceptible to that kind of thing. "If you want that, you'll find your way to it. You'll find your way to a good place with him again."

"Yes, but you see, with Theresa—"

"I'm telling you, Theresa's unimportant." I liked how sure Richard was. Like he knew. Like he knew her, and knew exactly how marginal that plaid living-room set was, ultimately. "All that's important is what's between the two of you, you and your husband."

"Yes, but what I feel is, because of how we began—" Those hot, sloppy kisses. Ignoring his cell phone when the mother of his children tried to call him. Lying left and right. How could we get past that? How could we ever move on from there?

"So begin again," Richard said, simply. A straightforward enough sentence, and quite appealing, as advice. What could it possibly mean, in practice? "Begin again with him, differently. It's never too late to do that. You can always find new ground."

And that, I guess, is the very definition of optimism, isn't it? It is never too late; you can always fix or change things, no stain is so black that it cannot be washed away. How I would have loved to believe it! How difficult it was for me to take that hope in—like passing a beautiful jewel in the shop window and thinking how glorious it is, how you'd adore to be lit up and sparkling with that particular glitter and color! But always the glass between you and the jewel, always the transparent, cold, non-negotiable glass: you can look but you cannot touch. You can want, but you cannot hold.

"I wish I knew how to do that," I told Richard. "I always get mired in the past. I don't know how to leave it behind. How do you do that? What's the trick? A person's history is always there. How are you supposed to pretend it doesn't exist?"

"It's not a question of pretending. It's just looking at what's between you and him *now*. What's happened has happened. You're not going to get anywhere trying to unhappen it." Well, that I liked. "You've got to just start from here, from now, and see where it goes."

There was that gesture toward the future again, and I couldn't help hearing this time in Richard's voice a darker layer of something, a sour slice right in there with the optimism. There was something else on the guy's mind, other than giving me his universal wisdom about how to fix my broken-down car of a life, of a marriage.

"And what about—" I began, cautiously. How to ask this? What did I want to say, actually? We were standing beside one another near Millie, still, and I sensed a restlessness coming on. There was something we were not talking about. (Not only that; we were both getting hungry. That raisin-bran muffin had been several revelations ago now.) I reached my hand into the fiery Pandora's box, the box of questions you're not sure you really want answers to. "What about you and me, here?" I asked. "How does that fit in?"

As the words were out of my mouth Richard reached for my hand, and sighed, and looked—for the first time since I'd met him—sad. And perhaps frustrated. His full, hopeful face, that turned always toward light and toward promise, wore for a moment a bleaker shade I knew all too well. *If only. I will never. We can't. How I wish.*

"This isn't what you want, Angel," Richard said to me, and on "this," he squeezed my hand tightly in his own large, strong paw. "I see that."

"What do you mean?" I squeaked, in a small mouse voice. Holding his hand tight, as if that might make up for the turned-away kiss. He had seen it; he had felt it, of course.

Richard tried to smile, but a frown maneuvered it out of the way, leaving a moistness in his eyes. "You've got somewhere to be." This was tidy common sense. Inarguable as a nine-by-twelve. "You've got people to look after."

"But—" I blurted. "But—I love you!"

He nodded. "I love you, too." He said this looking not at me, but at all the avenues of graves. The discreet, tactful trees. The fading flowers in bottles. Richard did not rush to smother or embrace me on our trading these proclamations. And the fact that he didn't, my beloved, stomach-rumbling friend, filled me with grief and relief, both. The 3 A.M. fantasies of our bodies together, Richard's and mine, were going to remain in their packaging, unopened, untested. It was clear. And the new black mark against my name, an act that would have required more deception, more lying, or else admission followed by condemnation and howls of rage, or of pain—there would not be any of that, either. No act, no black mark. Somewhere deep in my troubled, mottled self, a sigh. An escape. *Phew*. Got out of that one.

"There are plenty of different ways to love someone," Richard noted, and I could hear that he was talking not just to me, trying to help me through as he always did, giving me counsel, offering his solace; but that he was trying too to play that same role for himself. He was trying to make sense of what was unfolding in the *now*; and of what would never unfold in the *what's next*. "I can love you—and I always will—from a distance." It broke my heart to watch him. I wanted to give him some balm of my own, after all he had done for me! But I did not have the same gift as Richard. All I had was a nice smile, a pretty (if tear-streaked) face, and a big heart of affection within me that pumped the blood loudly through.

"But—" I said, searching for eloquence, finding none. "But—"

"I know." Still watching the graves, Richard nodded, brow furrowed, as if I had just made an interesting and insightful point. And then his face, like a sky, cleared abruptly. He was already looking to something else. Some new source of inspiration. No looking back, no regrets. No staying with the clouds. He was anticipating being somewhere else, somewhere it wouldn't hurt, where there would be no sense of loss. Richard was a fast traveler, in his way. A guy used to life on the road.

"I'm leaving," Richard told me, and his eyes met mine again, now that he had found a new expression. "That was why I had to see you today, to tell you. I'm going back to Chicago."

"For a trip? To see your mom?" I suddenly felt like the grabby and panicky one. These roles get reversed so quickly. Could I still change my mind? Should we kiss?

"No." Richard shook his head, as if in answer to all of the above. "I'm moving back. Some opportunities have arisen. Business opportunities. Too good to pass up."

"But what about the envelopes?" I could hear how ridiculous this sounded. As if those folding, sealable objects were his pets, or his children.

He kissed my hand, sweetly, then released it. Released *me*. He looked moved by my question. "Someone will look after the envelopes," he reassured. "Don't worry. The truth is it's not a business that needs the personal touch, really. I poured too much into it. My talents will be better used somewhere else." I thought of my husband's grim Internet searching, his discovery of Richard's alleged Chapter Eleven episode. I was glad not to know more of it: it was not a chapter of Richard's that I wanted to thumb through. I liked him best as the guy who calmed me and cared for me, who read me the runes. The idea of associating him with something as real and grubby as money was upsetting.

But there was another thing. "You used to say there was a purpose in our meeting," I said to Richard. I tried to keep a childish plaintiveness out of my tone. "What could the purpose have been, if you were just going to leave?"

Richard pondered. "Maybe it was to help you in your marriage. To guide you through."

"But that's so—selfless."

He shrugged, modestly. I found this theory hard to swallow. If that was all the universe was up to, surely it could have just sent me to an Internet site with free couples' counseling instead? Or tapped Puffin on the shoulder and told him to shape up?

"Well . . . " I couldn't think of what to say to him now. "I'll miss you." I didn't want to cry all over again. My face was steady now, salt-free, so I tried to keep what I said light. But true. I was not, at this moment, going to think deeply about how bereft I'd be without Richard. How thin the days would feel. How empty the fantasy-free nights.

"I'll miss you too, Angel." Richard's voice, too, stayed on the level. "Believe me, I'll miss you, too."

We embraced, but briefly, almost fearfully, stepping back from one another with speed. There was a shared need for movement. We both felt it. No good could come anymore of staying here among the dead. We had come to some sort of end of our own. Besides, there was this hunger to take care of.

"Let's go get a bite somewhere," Richard suggested, and I readily agreed. I whispered my private goodbye to Millie and we walked back down the path to return to the land of the living.

It was while heading downward that I felt, like a radioactive pellet in my pocket, the silver device that I had kept quiet for these hours. I remembered turning it off earlier, at the long-ago ferry terminal, but since Richard and I were in motion again it felt wrong to leave my lifeline unpowered, the voices it contained locked up.

"Do you mind," I asked Richard politely, "if I check my messages?"

"Go ahead!" He sounded quite cheerful, suddenly. Perhaps the thought of food encouraged him. I think we both needed grounding.

There were, my device informed me, eight voicemails waiting for me. It seemed a safe bet that they would all be from my spouse. "Oh dear," I said to Richard, who was a famished step ahead of me. "This won't be good." The coward in me, who on occasion takes up nearly my entire being, was loath to listen to each of the eight, reasoning that the mere fact of there being eight told me everything I needed to know, surely, about my husband's frenzy and upset. But then some better self nuzzled through, like a mole blindly digging toward daylight, and got me to listen to the whole progression of messages, while Richard walked ahead.

My husband started self-absorbed. The first message was a continuation of the DDT drama, which now seemed almost quaint, like a scratchy recording from another era. I noticed that he didn't apologize for having put me on hold to talk to her. This was message one: "So she was calling back, after all that, to say she wouldn't be able to get the boys from school today because 'something came up,' which probably just means she's pissed off and getting her nails done and wants to make us do it. So I said we would." Two: "Just wondering if you got Ryan to the boat all right, whether that all worked out. Let me know how it goes." Three was: "I'm beginning to get concerned that I can't reach you, and, you know, you've got the car, so I can't go anywhere, I'm kind of trapped here. Will you call me?" Four: "All right, I really need you to call me. I'm not sure why your phone is turned off. Let me know what's going on." (The former adulterer, here, beginning to get the sense that something is amiss. Beginning to nose the possibility that his wife is with someone else.) Five: "I've called the museum and managed to reach the teacher, so I know you got Ryan there. I don't know what game you're playing now. I'm asking you to call me, please." Here, in five, the anger was building. It was hard for me to hear it, and again I had to fight the impulse to put the silver device away altogether, but I tried to keep hold of my better mole self. It was keeping me brave. Six was evidently quite some time after five. Between five and six my husband had developed a plan, taken action. He was coming after me. Somehow he got himself down to the ferry terminal (by bus? friend? had Mike the former co-worker taken him?). Six was sharp, clipped with scarcely suppressed fury: "Don't take the boat back expecting to drive home from there. I've found the car and am taking it. I'm coming to the city." Sounding like a vigilante, powered by the spare set of keys.

"How about this place?" Richard called back to me, paused now in front of an adequate diner-like joint. Upmarket diner, that is: in this neck of the woods, nothing was ordinary. The fries would be made out of sweet potatoes or turnips, probably, and the meat for beef dishes from cows treated with kindness and grace.

"Looks good—I'll be in in a minute," I replied, not wanting to miss seven, which would presumably form a crucial part of the whole voicemail narrative. Richard waved back, relaxed, a *take your time* gesture. I loved that unhurried quality he had. I sat down on a bench by the diner, and heard how the rest of the husband story unfolded.

By seven the tone had taken a different turn altogether. Seven was desperate, tearful. "Listen," said seven, "I don't know what you're trying to do to me here. I found Ryan's class. The teacher explained—I know who you're with. I know what you're doing. But—but—what are you doing? Why can't you call me? I don't—I can't—" He broke there, the message ended, and I put a hand over my eyes. This man, my husband, did not, in spite of everything, deserve this. Yes, it was the case that he had once pulled a similar stunt on his spouse at the time—evading, escaping, ignoring his cell phone—but did that mean I was right to inflict the same torture on him now, these years later? Wasn't it God's job to punish him, not mine? What was I espousing here, an Old Testament morality, giving out to that once-errant man a lie for a lie, untruth for an untruth? Was that what I believed in? I thought about that other, opposite line—"Don't use people as a means to an end; treat every person as an end in himself." I had learned that in college: the virtue in looking *at* people, not through them. That is one good reason to go to college, to learn lines like that.

I wasn't sure I could bear message eight, but it was mercifully short, a morose, aged voice, simply imploring. "Please call me."

So I did, there on the bench. I called him.

The voice that fed through my small silver device was a dull echo of the voice I knew, and certainly a different character altogether from the one who had spoken first in the sequence, about DDT and the children.

"Hello?" my husband said hoarsely. The half question revealed little, but I knew he knew it was me calling: as I say, these cell phones take away all elements of surprise or suspense.

"Hi," I replied.

There was a pause. I wasn't sure how to start, here. Normally my husband is the kind to leap into a silence, he's not much of a one for dead air, but on this occasion he let the quiet swell like a balloon. Finally he just asked, "Yes?" like the grim guy waiting in the dock, sunken eyed, for the verdict to fall on his head.

I wasn't going to cry again. I had done my crying by Millie's gravestone already. But I did start to bleed, inwardly, at the wound I had inflicted. It's funny, that, isn't it? You slice someone else open, someone you love, and it's you who starts oozing.

"Sweetheart," I said to the small silver device, hoping it would feed the endearment through to the man I had once made all those public promises to. He had looked so good in his dark suit that day. He had been so proud, so jokeful, so capable of hope. And I had meant what I said to him. I had meant what I said.

"Come and get me. Let me explain where I am." I explained where I was. "I have plenty to tell you."

"Oh yeah?" my husband said, a decibel or two more volume in his voice now. But he was wary. "What kind of plenty? Good and plenty? Or bad and plenty?"

He was still able to kid around, that was a positive sign. "Tough but essential," I told my husband. "Like root-canal work." I might as well kid back. We had been good at that once, the two of us. "But here's what you need to know, first. I love you. And—" I might as well try this line for myself, see if I could pull it off. Reassure both of us. "Everything will be all right."

The House in the Clearing

Release — At a certain point, you have to let go.

This wisdom applies not just to you, but to the other people, too.

———✦———

I tottered into the diner to find Richard. He was at a corner table, holding half a hamburger in his hands, chewing, his face wearing the blank, satisfied expression of a person dousing his appetite. I felt something sharp, quick, in the vicinity of my heart or maybe my stomach: love, pity, regret—a slick knife, in and out. All these internal injuries I was enduring. It was like being in a car accident. Don't ever let anyone tell you infidelity, even near-miss infidelity, is easy on the innards. It isn't.

Richard looked apologetic when he saw me. "Sorry—I went ahead and ordered—" With a chivalrous gesture he indicated the seat across from him for me to sit in, and also that I should help myself to the heaped plate of multicolored fries (made from unusual root vegetables, taro and yam and the like, just as I'd predicted). But my stomach was now too jittery to accept anything like fries.

"My husband is coming," I told Richard in an odd, urgent blurt as I took my place. Seeing Richard there, my familiar lunching partner, this imminent spousal arrival seemed unreal and alarming. "To pick me up."

Richard nodded, unbothered. But his chewing slowed down. "Do you want me to leave?" He was, perhaps, remembering the natural disaster that occurred the last time the two men had met, and the state of emergency that was declared shortly afterward. We had all but qualified for federal aid, the three of us, after that scarring park-bench incident.

I looked away from my Irish good-luck charm and into a room full of high-end diners tucking in to their high-end diner food. I missed our falafel joint. I missed the posters of the Dead Sea and the Wailing Wall, I missed the Promised Land's tasty mixture of tahini and hummus, their warm, spongy pita wedges and the easy hour around all of it that Richard would fill with his observations and stories. We would never, it occurred to me, have one of those hours again. From now on, it was falafel on my own. Or with my husband. My stomach churned.

"No," I said to Richard. "Don't leave." *Ever. Please. I need you. How am I going to get through this without you?* "I don't see why you shouldn't finish your meal."

"Like a guy on death row, you mean?"

I smiled. "I think you may get a reprieve." I touched his arm. "And me, too. Let's hope. They're petitioning the governor's office right now for a stay of execution."

He raised his eyebrows, but I noticed he went on chewing. He had a dab of ketchup on the tip of his moustache and I reached across to wipe it off with my thumb, without thinking. I realized what an intimate gesture it was, and I put my forehead in my shuddering hand, to shield my stinging eyes from the world and enjoy a welcome moment of darkness. I still wanted something from this man. Maybe I'd never know exactly what it was—companionship; Zen blessings; sensual, adulterous bliss; stories about sandwiches—but in any case it did not matter, because I was never going to get it. Any of it. He was leaving. Did he understand how sad this was?

I uncovered my eyes again and faced him. "Tell me," I begged Richard. "Tell me some of your stories."

And so, amiably, he did, in the long minutes before my husband arrived. He told me a funny one about the butter-carving contest at the Illinois State Fair, when the woman who won created a magnificent all-dairy John Deere tractor. He told me about an aunt of his who lived in Streator, Illinois, a place which called itself the Glass Container Capital of the World. He mentioned that Lake Michigan was so big you could imagine it an ocean, and wonder if whales lived secretly deep within it. And somehow that led to a story about an evening he had amused Sarah, his stepdaughter, by fishing for ice cubes from her drink with an elaborate rod fashioned from toothpicks, and by the time he was winding up that tale my husband was there in the diner and my gamble was in action, that in a busy public place my husband would not make a scene. It was not as though he was a mobster likely to spray the place with machine-gun fire. (Or so I believed.) As my overworked coronary organ hammered and pounded, I simply stood up, like a good hostess, and gestured from one man to the other, saying, "Richard, this is my husband Alan, Alan—Richard Applebee."

Richard put out a hand he wiped off first, saying, "Pleased to meet you, Alan," and my husband, after a deliberate pause, returned the handshake, though his lips curled like burning paper at the clasp and he merely grunted, did not attempt any fiction like *the pleasure is all mine.*

Nonetheless. We got through that moment without anyone shrieking or dying, and that seemed to me progress. Richard, who though calm had gone a paler shade of Irish, could see that in the most literal way there was no room at the table for my husband, so he threw his napkin down onto his plate like a flag of surrender, stood up, and offered Alan his chair. "Here—" he said. "Why don't you sit? I was just getting ready to leave."

First, though, my husband leaned over me, with his tall, possessive frame, and planted a definitive kiss on my mouth. He might as well have shouted it: *Hands off, everybody! This one belongs to me.* It embarrassed me, there in the diner, but I knew he felt he had to mark the territory, and I figured I did not have the right to protest. People say men are dogs, and I would tend to agree on the basis of this experience, though I'm not sure I mean it the way other people do. Alan stepped away from me and looked at Richard, eye for an eye, as they stood a couple of feet apart.

"She's an angel, isn't she?" my husband said, his voice edged with threat, and he and Richard and I all knew who he was quoting.

"She is," Richard replied with dignity. "Yes, she is." Then he excused himself to find the cash register or the bathroom or someplace, any place, in the restaurant where there might be some oxygen. He seemed somewhat short of breath.

This left my husband and me facing each other across a table in a restaurant that pretended to be ordinary but wasn't, pricewise, in this town at the foot of the mountain. We had never been in this place together. We had not traveled as widely as we might have. I wondered if it was time for that to change.

The superior, growling expression that my husband had worn to chase Richard away subsided, and for a moment he looked at me and was very nearly the Alan I had first met: hesitant, cappuccino in hand, wondering if he would get very far with this mad tea-drinking scribbler.

"Are you in love with him?" my husband asked me. The hoarse, gray voice. Like a pale old raven. The eyes probing and haunted.

I shook my head. "No." I wondered whether this was true. I didn't honestly know, but it seemed clear that it was the right way to answer the question. "I care about him, though. He's—he's someone I care about."

My husband nodded, his lips pressed tight together. This was not good news for him, but it was not the worst news, either.

"And—" I might as well tell Alan something he would like to hear. "He's moving away. Back to Chicago. He's leaving the area."

Before my husband had a chance to absorb or react to that news the envelope guy himself reappeared, as if stage-managed, to produce his keen parting line. He was holding his wallet and his deck of cards and saying, hastily, "I'd better go now. I've settled the bill for my meal. I'll leave you two here." I, stalling, flustered, stood and offered Richard a ride, wondering how he would get anywhere from there—as if Alan would really agree to chauffeur around this man he had once referred to as a bulbous clown, and would as soon whack with a hatchet. If those men were in a car together, there was no good way to predict what might happen; the image of one of the three of us at the bottom of the bay sleeping with the fishes cut across my imagination, and I dare say theirs too. Richard, in any case, was quick-witted enough to refuse my idiotic offer, insisting that he had friends nearby who could take him in and get him to wherever he needed to go next. Who could say? Perhaps he did have friends who lived near there; sometimes when Richard talked it seemed as if he had friends all over, people who gave him their cars or their couches to borrow for one night or ten. Who knew anything about Richard, really, and how he got anywhere? The man was a nomad, it seemed, as well as a leprechaun, who appeared magically, spreading joy and relief, and then disappeared just as suddenly to disperse his stories and wisdom elsewhere.

My leprechaun. Would I ever see him again after today? I could not even kiss or embrace him here in front of my husband, who needless to say was tracking every movement with the alert, slitted eyes of a cat, so Richard and I had to settle for an arm clasp from a distance, to acknowledge our separation. There was one fleeting butterfly moment of our eyes meeting, when those soul windows opened wordlessly onto our mutual love and affection. And then he was gone, with his cards and his philosophies. I almost expected to see a puff of smoke where he had just been.

But instead there was my husband, and a used, half-broken marriage that needed some repair work, along with a depleted plate of French fries made with strange vegetables, and a glass of half-melted ice water with random bits of debris floating in it. It was an unappetizing scene.

"Well—" Alan began, and I could see from his lean, edged face, which had lifted some in the wake of Richard's departure, that he was going to chase the image of the large red-bearded man further away with some form of disparagement. "He certainly—"

"*Don't.*" There was a cool authority in my voice that stopped him. It was the tone I had to pull out sometimes for Ryan or Alan— the younger Alan that is—if they were doing, or about to do, something absolutely beyond the pale. "Just—don't."

He sat back, chastened. Waiting. I had his attention, though.

"Be careful, here," I continued. It was odd, as though someone were ventriloquizing through me, an outside puppeteer who could change my character, after all those years, from mealy-mouthed, self-loathing accepter of indignities and forced kitchen labor to a woman who had, finally, had enough, and was not afraid to say so. Wasn't there some terrible horror movie in the seventies in which a girl got possessed by an evil spirit who started speaking in a low, monstrous voice through her? I was something like that girl. Taken over. Delivering my long-suppressed truth.

"If this is going to work, Alan, certain things will have to be different," I stated. As though someone had written the lines for me, and I was reading from a teleprompter right behind his head. "*You will have to leave Theresa.*"

"But—"

"She's not your wife anymore, and you're not her husband, and you can't let her keep acting otherwise."

"But—"

"I've finally figured it out: I'm not interested in bigamy. You can stay with Theresa, and keep having your negotiations over money and video games and whatever else you both come up with to keep each other engaged, or you can come with me. That," I told Alan, "is your choice to make."

"But the boys—"

"The boys are not served by all your self-indulgent squabbling." I was surprised I had this in me, but part of my self was standing to one side, impressed. Go ahead! Let him have it! Tell him what's what, after all this time. "The way you two constantly call each other to discuss the shuttlings of the boys keeps them trapped in this miserable divorce limbo, year after year. Those children would be far better off with the divisions clear between you. And then, you know, she would even be free, Theresa would be, to finally move on. She's holding, she's clinging—she has never let *go*. She uses the boys as an excuse to hang on. Look at her! She still can't even see me, or say my name." It had been one of the more successful erasures of all these years, Theresa keeping me nameless. "That is over," I said. It seemed to bear repeating. "That is over. If you want us to stay married."

"Or you'll go off with—with—" Alan gestured toward the place where the puff of smoke might have been. He could not say Richard's name, anymore than Theresa could say mine. He choked on it.

"Or I'll go," I affirmed, but I wasn't going to pin the departure on Richard. Richard was, in any case, already gone. He was going to Chicago, where he would be exploring new business opportunities. "Right. Or I'll go."

"Did you two want to see the menu again?" came a chirpy voice at Alan's elbow. "Would you like to order more food?"

"Actually," my husband said with surprising, uncharacteristic politeness to the waitress, "I think we're all done here. I'd like—" This to me, but his tone was gentle, conciliatory, "I'd like to get some air."

We packed up our small individual kits of money and identity—phones, wallets, keys—and left the high-end diner behind. Alan did not try to steer me, this time, on the way out. I think he had temporarily lost his confidence that I was his belonging. His vessel. He might have to let me pilot myself for a while.

Outside, the rain had started. It was not yet a deluge, it was still the first-speed-of-wiper-blades type of rain, maybe even just intermittent. The sky was mottled gray and the mountain was now hiding, and the limbs of the oaks on the hills were turning wet black, their small green leaves darkening. From somewhere came the smell of bay leaves, the distinctive forest scent of this area, and I had the sense, as you do in some of those expensive, on-the-edge neighborhoods, that the country was still around us; that the million-dollar houses were, after all, thin shelters, constructions of faith or of hubris, when what was most powerful about the place was just a few striding yards away, upwards. Woods, brush, and creeks; snakes, deer, and raccoons: all the wild world awaited. I breathed in its air, and its air fed me deeply. I had been inhaling such canned, urban stuff for so long now, the air in and around our condo.

"Sometimes," I told Alan, as we walked slowly in the gathering rain, and the water was like a pat on the back, a stroke on the cheek, in its sweetness, "I wish I could live here again."

There was a silence, and I realized as I looked at him what was different about my husband. He was listening. It would have been perfectly in keeping with Alan's past record to issue some satirical comment about this town and its residents, but he refrained.

"I know it's impossible," I added, moved by his quiet. "I'm just saying. This was my home, once." And though my life by the mountain had had its share of shocks and letdowns, of course, when I'd lived here I had never imagined there would be a DDT in my future. I had never thought about how far down you could get dragged by marital circumstances.

He reached for my hand in the rain. This was not Richard, big Richard, looking ahead and feeling cheerful, not knowing me but loving me, mostly I suppose on the basis of my nice smile, which has over the years persuaded plenty of people of virtues I may or may not possess. No, no. This was my husband holding my hand now; Alan, the sturdy, gentlemanly man I had married, who had always been, in spite of the bitter ex-wife and enemy meter maids, a man with a good heart and a nice hand at wordplay, some of the reasons why I had said yes in the first place. He never meant to shout, rant, cause harm. He had meant to be a decent sort. To take care. I knew that was how he had intended to be. I believed he was unaware of the person he had become.

"I'm sorry." He sighed, from deep within. All the way in there. "I am so, so sorry."

And there are sorrys and there are sorrys. There are sorrys that have implied within them, But it wasn't really my fault, or, I couldn't help it. There are sorrys that are quick and snappy, meaning, OK, but let's not linger on all that, can we move on now? There are sorrys that are forced and sulky, I'll say this because you're making me, let it be recorded that I have said *sorry*, though damned if I really am. There are sorrys that are issued only as part of a trade, Well, I may be sorry but by all rights you ought to be a hell of a lot sorrier, and now it's your turn, buddy, let's hear it. There are I'm sorrys that really mean I hate you, or, I'm kidding, or, I didn't hear you, or, If there's one thing I'm not, it's sorry. There are all those kinds of sorrys and probably some others I'm forgetting. Someone should make a wall chart. Maybe there'll be multiple entries in my dictionary.

Then there is the real thing.

Alan meant his sorry. I could feel remorse motoring through him, and the remorse was running on a fuel I had stopped hoping Alan would ever fill up on, namely comprehension. For the first time in five years, it seemed, there in the rain, he got it. He understood what had happened to me in the course of our marriage. It wasn't only he who had been inconvenienced by DDT's rages and engagements; his current wife, the second one, old whatsername, *me*—I'd had a lacerating time of it too. If there had been something Alan and Theresa had in common for that whole five-year stretch, it sometimes occurred to me, it was their ongoing failure to consider the one or three other people around who might be affected by their drama.

"It wasn't pretty," he acknowledged, "the way I left her."

"No," I agreed. "It was never pretty."

There was a pause, as we both recollected the lack of prettiness there had been.

"I'm sorry," he said again, for emphasis.

I squeezed his hand in reply. There is nothing to say back to the wholehearted apology. It's not a question of, Oh, that's OK! Don't worry about it. Or even, Thank you—though I would, some time later, thank him. It is necessary to leave the space wide open around the words, first, for them to gather their intent, their meaning. It was important, in this instance, to take a few, long breaths of acceptance. So I did. I breathed. I held his hand. I made sure he knew I was with him.

"I thought about what Puffin said." Alan's voice was subdued. Until now he had not, since that thankless post-Thanksgiving meeting on the therapist's stage set, mentioned it. "About the unreal promises."

I nodded.

"I should never, I guess, have said that thing about keeping you like a key."

"And," I pointed out, "I've always been too big to fit inside your pocket."

"It's true." Alan unclasped our hands for a moment to brush off his face—the rain or some other liquid, perhaps some thin sheen of shame. "I have not been able to make you safe, or happy. It's terrible to admit that. I tried to, I tried to make you happy, but—"

"There's still warm, though."

"What?"

" 'Safe, warm and happy,' you used to say. That still leaves warm, even if we forget about safe or happy."

Alan looked at me, his brow raised. He understood that we were playing here a little, again. "You think I could manage that?" he asked. "To keep you warm?"

"I do." I smiled at him, as I hadn't in a long while. "I do think you could manage that."

He reached for my hand again. "Goddamn heating bills, though." He shook his head. He was making fun of himself, at last. What a relief. "I don't know. Maybe we can go with something low cost. Sleeping bags. Blankets."

"Body warmth. That's the simplest."

"There you go."

We walked on for a bit in a more companionable silence. We were getting there. Slowly, we were getting somewhere. I felt a strange, unfamiliar prickling sensation, and slowly recognized it as *hope*.

The street my husband and I were strolling along was residential. We were putting distance between ourselves and the craft nooks, the trinketerías, the taro French fries. We were in an area in which the driveways were long and the security systems good-looking, but we were not, around there, near the special, gated hideaways of millionaires. We were low enough down that the lives on display were still in the imaginable range.

"It isn't impossible, you know."

This was my husband, Alan, and he was speaking to me. Not at me, but to me.

"What do you mean?"

"It isn't impossible." He wasn't letting go of my hand now, though our grips were getting slicker as the precipitation made itself felt. "We could move."

"I beg your pardon?" It was as though the man were speaking in tongues. I couldn't understand him.

"I mean we could get out of that condo. We could move. I lost my job, obviously, and—I don't know, maybe I'm wrong about this, but I don't see you spending the rest of your life in that sta-tionery store."

I gave him a sideways look before replying. "I could take time away from stationery, it's true. All those demanding customers. All that standing still."

"All those envelopes," Alan said, and I found that somehow funny and subtle, and I didn't mind it so much. "You could do with a rest from the envelopes, in particular."

"Perhaps."

"Finkelstein called the house, by the way, this morning. While you were . . . " Alan looked up into the rain for a moment, blinked at the drops falling on him. "While you were out. So I told him you'd had an urgent family matter to take care of, and wouldn't be coming in."

"Thank you."

"No problem. He said he hoped everything was OK, but that he'd really need you tomorrow because the Valentine's Day crap, excuse me, merchandise, is beginning to pour in."

A life without Mr. Finkelstein, and the forthcoming cards cov-ered in hearts and roses, which would soon be followed by eggs and bunnies, then floral Mother's Day appreciations—the whole seasonal coding of our predestined sentiments for one another—could I manage without all that? It was contemplatable. Mr. Finkelstein had been an anchor, in his way, but it was true, too, that if I had to forge ahead now without Richard around to brighten the place, I might find it difficult to enjoy, in the old spirit, the long taciturn hours with my boss.

"But—" I focused more clearly on what Alan was suggesting. Leaving the stationery store I could see, yes, and he had lost his job, yes, but wasn't there another part of the picture here? Weren't there two other parts of the picture, to be precise? "What about the boys?"

Alan let the gathering rain speak for a minute before he replied. You have to understand that this guy was a talker, not a thinker: he had never been, generally, someone to leave patches of serene silence about the place, if he had the chance to scatter them with his words and his noise. That he was keeping so quiet now was some indication of internal revolution. Leopards don't change their spots, I knew that even before I had stepchildren and read all those tales likening people to animals, but it is possible, under duress, for a man used to drowning out objections or questions with his bluster to decide to take a break from the production of commentary and reaction. And, when he does, for surprising new thoughts to make their way into the conversation.

"There could be a different arrangement with the boys," Alan said, finally. "You know—weekends. Vacations. Maybe that would work better."

I felt like an animal trainer who had spent five years trying to coax an extremely shy and untamed idea out of its underground warren, and here it was at last, showing the tip of its nose in the light. *The idea of moving away from Theresa, from their former house, from the boys, the divorce, and the bitterness.* If I moved or breathed, the idea might dash back inside and I would never see it again.

"That might work," I all but whispered. "Yes. It just might."

"Is that what you want? Sweetheart?"

On hearing that question, apparently, the clouds drew themselves together. They were deciding to storm, properly. They were getting ready to open up the heavens. And there's that point when rain turns from soft, cleansing shower, metaphoric purifier and friend, into something more aggressive, pneumonia-inducer, puddle-former, traffic-jammer. We were heading toward the latter.

"Look, the car's just ahead up there. We're almost to where I parked. Let me get the umbrella out of there or you're going to get soaked. It's the least I can do," my husband said, "to try to keep you warm." And Alan left me with the downpour beginning seriously to pour down on me while he, thoughtful fellow, extracted from the car that thin, many-tined protection against the elements. He came back promptly, and much as I enjoyed the free gifts of the atmosphere—I'm the earth, air, fire, water type—I was just as glad, at this key juncture, to huddle with my husband, no longer exposed.

He had parked the car in a side street, not far from a small house that was set back a ways from the road. It was not like some of the other houses around there: it was neither low modern nor mock-Tudor, not an ornate villa nor a geodesic dome. Whoever designed it had not tried hard to think outside the box. It was just a small, ordinary house with the sort of simple, unassuming garden that someone with black thumbs, like me, can respond to. It had a clearing around it, this house, the feeling that it was its own humble, private dwelling that could invite others in when it chose to, but might live most of its days quietly. It looked like you could be comfortable within it: calm, taken care of, but with room to move about freely. And the opportunity, if you opened wide the windows, to inhale the smells of the mountain, the bay.

"Something like this." I pointed toward the house, as if my husband, Alan, could possibly know what I meant. "That's what I want."

Alan frowned, intently. He was listening. Even if he found me mysterious, inscrutable, his face indicated that he was going to try his damnedest to figure me out. I appreciated that. It might not come naturally between my husband and me, in all respects— understanding, that is, the free, wordless exchange between souls—but he was planning to make the effort. He wanted to work out how to look after me. Richard had scared my husband, had spooked him, into recalling those promises he had made in front of that small gathered crowd that had included, let's not forget, my mother. Alan seemed belatedly to remember that he was once a man who had had rice thrown over him, on camera, while wearing a dark suit, in proximity to me in my gold gown. He had called me a wonder. Had considered himself a lucky man.

He was listening.

"A house—a home," I explained, raising my voice against the rain's thrum on the umbrella overhead and the sidewalk around us. I couldn't expect my husband to read my mind. For better or for worse. Rice or no rice. "A home with a kettle, and a stove, and a refrigerator, and no photographs around. Let's skip the photographs for a while. A telephone that does not get answered every time it rings, if you and I are home together, alone. A card table in the corner for Monopoly, or homework, or gin rummy. Do you know how to play gin rummy?"

He shook his head apologetically.

"That's all right. I'll teach you. Someone very close to me taught me how to play when I was a kid. Did I ever tell you about Millicent Larsen?"

"Maybe. I'm not sure."

"Well, if I did, I'll tell you again. Remind me. She's important. There are—" I took a deep breath, and exhaled. "There are important things to tell you."

I kept going. We could have gotten into the car at that point, to get out of the weather, but Alan could tell I was on a roll, that I had to finish the sequence before we could go anywhere. This, too, was new. Normally the man wore impatience like a second skin, and would have hustled me into the car so we could move on to the next thing. There were children to be collected later in the day, as neither of us had forgotten. But instead of pressing the point, my husband waited beside me.

"And I want to go on vacations, occasionally," I continued, "to places you have never been with Theresa. And I want to quit making jokes about her van and calling her DDT. And I want, once in a while, to go to the movies, just Ryan and me, because he's a great kid and I think we have similar senses of humor."

My husband nodded. This all seemed manageable, so far, I guess.

"And I want to start writing again." This I said less brashly, in a more muted tone. "I'd like to return to my Dictionary of Betrayal."

Alan weighed this, amidst the wet drumbeats. "You've got some new material," he commented dryly. "That should help you get back into it."

"I certainly do." I appreciated his noticing. "There will be plenty of pages to fill in." The Universe and its workings; Zen lines; Scenes from a cemetery. "Maybe you'd care to read some of it, finally? After all of this time?"

"I might. I just might."

"Though there are not, I should warn you, a whole lot of police-procedural elements in there."

"I can cope. Don't worry."

I was going to carry on and sketch the rest out for him, how I'd be there in the hushed study, writing, while he went off to his new job at the Something or Other Company, where he did finances, or consulting, or maybe both together—perhaps at long last I'd come to understand it—and where the co-workers would be open-faced and agreeable and the management fair-minded. How we would never get parking tickets or discuss city government or spend entire dinners rehashing alimony payments. How I planned to cash in on all those as-yet-undelivered backrubs in front of movies that had more to do with love and conversation than global spy networks and intricate heists gone wrong.

But, really, why spell all of that out, now? We could fill in the details, as and when. Alan had gotten the gist.

So I kissed him, instead of continuing my list, and if it wasn't the hottest, sloppiest kind of kiss it was nonetheless full and true, and it told my husband something. Something he needed to hear.

And then we were ready to climb back into our safe haven of a car together. We made ourselves comfortable in its worn leather interior. Alan turned on the ignition and flicked on the wipers, which gave us the road ahead of us, back and forth, wiped clean, over and over again, by the slick blade.

"Now where?" my husband asked me, considerately, as the car's engine slowly warmed us, and I thought to myself: What an interesting question.

Bodies at rest — There is no shame—in fact, there is no betrayal—in recovering, finally, your peace of mind. Those wakeful small hours, whether live with fire or with fury, were soul lacerations, all.

Quiet, somnolent nights have much to recommend them. Two can sleep side by side more easily than three.

ACKNOWLEDGMENTS

This novel comes straight from the dark solitary heart of the middle of the night. However, there are friends and colleagues who helped bring it into the light—I would like to thank, for early encouragement and conversation, Ann Packer and Geri Thoma; for her delightful illuminations, and a willingness to share them, Monica Scott; for thoughtful readings and response, Peggy Orenstein, Kate Moses, Ayelet Waldman, Ann Cummins, Nancy Johnson, Mary Pols and Maia Ettinger; for the leap of faith, Jack Shoemaker; for careful attention to the words themselves, and to the shape of my story, Sam Humphreys; for a steady hand and a good voice, Pat Kavanagh. Finally, for patience and understanding, I'd like to thank my first reader, my companion, my mate—Sedge Thomson.